"Happy birthday to me."

I had not yet forgiven Collin for ruining my birthday, but I had begun to realize that if I were facing something I really didn't want to do, I would rather have Mom arguing for me than Daddy.

"Collin still has a chance," Mom said. "Boys who come home unable to dress themselves or walk the dog don't have another chance. Their parents can be feeding a grown man like a baby and taking him to the bathroom, and wondering who will do that for him when they're too old, or have died. Is that what you want for us?"

Daddy held up a piece of mail. "This conversation isn't about what we want. He's supposed to show up for duty."

Mom looked shaken. "His draft notice?"

"It's time for Collin to grow up and be a man," Daddy said, standing up to leave the table.

"I want him to live long enough to be one," Mom said, dropping her fork on the plate.

I was the only one left at the table after that.

The candles had not been lit.

Happy birthday to me.

Summer's End

AUDREY COULOUMBIS

speak

An Imprint of Penguin Group (USA) Inc.

SPEAK
Published by the Penguin Group
Penguin Group (USA) Inc.,
345 Hudson Street, New York, New York 10014, U.S.A.
Penguin Group (Canada), 90 Eglinton Avenue East, Suite 700,
Toronto, Ontario,Canada M4P 2Y3 (a division of Pearson Penguin Canada Inc.)
Penguin Books Ltd, 80 Strand, London WC2R 0RL, England
Penguin Ireland, 25 St Stephen's Green, Dublin 2, Ireland
(a division of Penguin Books Ltd)
Penguin Group (Australia), 250 Camberwell Road, Camberwell, Victoria 3124, Australia
(a division of Pearson Australia Group Pty Ltd)
Penguin Books India Pvt Ltd, 11 Community Centre,
Panchsheel Park, New Delhi - 110 017, India
Penguin Group (NZ), Cnr Airborne and Rosedale Roads,
Albany, Auckland 1310, New Zealand (a division of Pearson New Zealand Ltd)
Penguin Books (South Africa) (Pty) Ltd, 24 Sturdee Avenue,
Rosebank, Johannesburg 2196, South Africa

Registered Offices: Penguin Books Ltd, 80 Strand, London WC2R 0RL, England

First published in the United States of America by G. P. Putnam's Sons,
a division of Penguin Young Readers Group, 2005
Published by Speak, an imprint of Penguin Group (USA) Inc., 2007

10 9 8 7 6 5 4 3 2 1

THE LIBRARY OF CONGRESS HAS CATALOGED THE G. P. PUTNAM'S SONS EDITION AS FOLLOWS:
Couloumbis, Audrey. Summer's end / Audrey Couloumbis.
p. cm.   Summary: Three teenaged cousins worry about their uncle who is missing in
Vietnam, their brothers—the one who was drafted and the two
who are dodging the draft, and the effects of their absence on the four
generations gathered at the family farm in the summer of 1965.
1. Vietnamese Conflict, 1961–1975—Juvenile fiction. [1. Vietnamese Conflict,
1961–1975—Fiction. 2. Draft resisters—Fiction. 3. Farm life—Fiction.
4. Family life—Fiction.] I. Title.
PZ7.C8305 Su 2005   [Fic]—dc22   2004058655
ISBN: 0-399-23555-8 (hc)

Speak ISBN 978-0-14-240783-7

Printed in the United States of America

We each owe one life,
*   but there are many who pay a higher price.*

To mothers and fathers everywhere
*   in the hope that history will not forever repeat itself.*

Contents

1 SOME OLD BUSYBODY

The day before my thirteenth birthday, my big brother, Collin, went to one of those hippie sit-ins. Where he and some likewise stupid boys torched their draft cards.

That draft card was pretty much Collin's invitation to join the army. He wasn't supposed to turn the invitation down, much less burn it. The way we found out, some old busybody called to tell Daddy he ought to truck on over there to the junior college and skin Collin's sorry tail.

Told Daddy Collin was going to get himself arrested in a hot minute. Yelled so loud, Daddy couldn't hold the phone to his ear. Everything she said carried real well.

Daddy slammed down the phone. "I've got to see for myself what's going on out there," he said.

"I'll go with you, Daddy." I peeled my sweaty self off the couch and brushed away fuzzy bits of tweed that were stuck to my legs.

"No, Grace," he said, already on his way out of the house. "You stay here."

The screen door swung back with a squeal of the spring. I caught it and stepped out onto the porch, feeling left out. It used to be Daddy took me with him everywhere. Lately, he was always mad about something.

Collin's dog, a big white Lab, was hot on Daddy's heels as he crossed the yard, trying to lick his hand. Daddy didn't want to play. He yelled, "Call this dog back to you."

I made a halfhearted effort. "Caboose."

Daddy aimed a kick at the bright spot of lime green on the truck's rear gate, where Mom once stuck a peace sign. Daddy had scratched off as much of it as he could. He turned around and pointed his finger at me. "Call off your party too."

"Noooo," I said. I stamped my foot. If this wasn't just typical. Collin got his party, and then he goes and ruins mine. He couldn't pick a better time for this? It's not like anybody had ever made a secret of the fact that boys get drafted.

Daddy got in the truck and pointed his finger at me again. The Finger of Doom, my friend Judy called it. She could afford to make jokes. It never got pointed at her. She never got punished for something Collin did.

Daddy drove off with a squeal of tires, the dog running hard behind the truck. Like the dog, I was not giving up that easily. I let the screen door bang shut behind me and went through the house to tell Mom.

It took me three weeks of begging to get her okay for this party. She kept telling me I was too old for a birthday party. What was she trying to say? Just because this was my only birthday party since I was six years old did not mean I had outgrown them.

Practically the whole twelfth grade came to our house for Collin's graduation party. I only got to invite half my class, but my birthday party could be just as good. If I got any cooperation at all.

It was a good thing a party with boys didn't need silly party favors, only a dance floor and plenty of soda pop. We still had the dance floor Daddy built, standing on its edge in the garage. But I needed music. I had to get permission to use my own money.

"Could we talk about my party?" I would ask at suppertime. "I'd like to buy some new records."

"I thought you bought new records last week," Daddy said.

"I need to have the latest ones for my party."

"You made up your own mind how much money you wanted to set aside for saving, didn't you?" Daddy said. He was right, but in the first rush of enthusiasm, I had been too strict with myself.

"Maybe you could ask some of your friends what they have," Mom said, knowing I didn't have any more spending money. She'd told me I had to get Daddy's okay to use my savings. "Borrow some records for one day," she said. "That's what Collin did."

"Collin's girlfriend has every record the minute it comes out," I said. "He didn't have to borrow—Kerrie simply put herself in charge of the music."

"The boys aren't going to dance at this party anyway," Daddy said then. If his voice could write on stone, that line would have been added to the Ten Commandments. "Boys your age are too shy of girls."

"Daddy."

He pointed that finger at me. "You are way too young to be giving that kind of party."

That was how the birthday talks went. First Mom told me I was too old for a birthday party, then Daddy told me I was too young to dance with a boy. There was not one person in the world who cared if I ever had a fun time.

"Could I be excused?" I'd say. "I have to see if anybody else has some new records." Pardon me while I humiliated myself, calling around and borrowing things.

That was the begging. There was a bargain too. Mom said I had to vacuum the whole house the day before and the day after the party. I'd do the vacuuming and she'd make me a cake.

Collin did not have to beg or bargain or borrow for his party. He didn't have to do anything but mow the lawn, which was his job anyway. He didn't have to help with cleanup either. I know, because I did.

But we made a deal, Mom and me. I had already done the before. I had vacuumed the entire house, plus cleaned the bathroom. She threw the bathroom in at the last minute. That birthday party was all set—I couldn't call it off.

I found Mom in the little shed where she worked, painting roses on this old buffet. She was leaning in close, getting paint in her hair as she concentrated on some small detail. Right up till then I'd hoped she'd see my side of things. But the minute I saw her, I knew it wouldn't happen that way at all. This thing with Collin was too big.

"Grace, where did your daddy go?" she asked me.

"Somebody called. They said Collin burned his draft card."

"Oh, no." Mom sat back. She threw her paintbrush down on her worktable, saying, "I hope your daddy can bring him on home."

I asked, "Do you think Collin will get arrested?" Because burning draft cards is against the law. I knew this because Daddy and Collin had completely destroyed a Sunday afternoon arguing about it being a form of free speech.

"Don't say it," Mom said, pushing her hair away from her face. "Don't even think about it."

I did think about it. Things had not been right around here since Collin started acting up. He let his hair grow to his shoulders. Painted peace signs on his jeans. He wanted to go to sit-ins and such over at the junior college with our cousin Thatcher.

"Not on your life," Daddy had said the first time Collin asked.

"My life," Collin said. "Exactly."

That was how they'd been talking to each other lately, in very few words.

"It was just a sit-in," Mom said in a bewildered way.

I knew what she meant. Collin went to a sit-in last week and nothing like this happened.

She asked, "Do you know who it was that called?"

"I think it was Mrs. Miller from the drugstore."

There was nothing going on that that woman didn't make it her business to know about. If we held an election to throw somebody out of town, Mrs. Miller would win hands down.

2 With No Warning

I'd seen sit-ins on TV lots of times. Definition of a sit-in: lots of kids my brother's age, sitting around on lawns like they were at a picnic. Standing around holding signs they'd made themselves. Smiling into the camera and holding up two fingers in a V that meant "peace."

It looked like somebody got a bunch of kids together to do a play but forgot to give them any lines. They had to make up their own. They made their costumes out of old clothes with patches, like Halloween tramps.

Then some college kids in Ohio got shot for having a sit-in. I didn't know such a thing could happen. We were all four of us sitting in the living room during the news report, the smell of lilacs coming in the open windows. I waited for a clue—how were we supposed to act? But no one said anything.

I said, "I thought sit-ins were commercials for higher education." I had used those words, *higher education,* the way my teachers used them.

Mom and Daddy went on staring at the TV. Collin looked at me the way he had been looking at me just lately—like I'd said something stupid.

Because of that look, I felt stupid. My face burned with embarrassment.

He said, "Those people are protesting the war in Vietnam."

"Being a big brother goes to your head sometimes, doesn't it?" I said. "You get to believing you always knew things like that."

"It must be nice," he said, "when you know people are dying and it doesn't have to matter."

Which was pure meanness. I felt that remark right in my heart.

Daddy got up and turned off the TV. He said, "We're just one big happy family around here."

"You can't mean to ignore what happened to those kids at Kent State," Collin had said to Daddy then. Collin looked at Mom and said, "Don't you see how wrong this is?"

Mom was still staring at the dark TV. Mom stared this way whenever she had to make up her mind about something. I had never gotten the feeling this meant she was thinking, so much as she was waiting. We'd all been doing a lot of waiting.

The month before this, Uncle Sawyer, who was in Vietnam, had gone down in a helicopter in enemy territory. The army called this "missing in action." Their lingo for lost, just plain lost and nobody knew where.

As if that wasn't bad enough, my cousin Dolly's brother, Willie, had been shipped over there back when there was snow on the ground. Now we had lilacs in bloom, and no one had even heard of the place he'd been sent.

"What's wrong with college kids going to war?" Daddy said when Mom didn't answer Collin. "If there's no draft, only poor kids and farm boys will ever go."

"What's wrong is people are dying," Collin said. "Kids are getting shot right here at home."

"They aren't kids anymore," Daddy said.

"Then why can't they vote?" Collin asked. "They never even had a say in this. If they aren't kids anymore, then why should they have to act like they're being told it's bedtime, go to their rooms?"

Daddy told Collin to go to his room.

Collin left the house and didn't come back till after the late news. But before he left, I could see it all over him that he wanted to protest the war too. Only Daddy wouldn't let him.

After that day, it was Kent State this and Kent State that. People talked about it everyplace we went—to school, to church, to the post office.

Then it happened again in Mississippi. College kids got shot at a sit-in.

There was another big blowup at our house. When the smoke cleared, Mom had made up her mind. She said Collin's own daddy had died in the Korean War, she thought he had the right to say whatever he wanted to about this one.

She told Collin he could go over to the junior college to hold up a sign.

I was amazed. She didn't want him to go to war in case he got killed, but she would let him go to a sit-in? Hadn't she just seen how kids got shot for doing that?

Which was pretty much what Daddy had to say about the matter. "It's too dangerous now. Don't rock the boat—that's the lesson we ought to be learning here," he said.

Mom's face flushed, the way it did when she was mad. But she looked away from Daddy. Instead of loud and angry, her voice sounded small, helpless. "I don't like the idea any better than you do," she told him, "but I can't say no to him over this."

"I'll say no to him," Daddy said.

"No, you won't," Mom said, and her voice didn't sound helpless anymore.

So you could say that even before Collin's little bonfire, we pretty much had a fight in every room. There was no time when everybody agreed about one thing except maybe what was on our dinner plates.

Mom and I waited on the front porch swing. When Daddy got back from the junior college, he pulled into the driveway with a scratch of gravel. I saw right away he'd come home alone. The tops of the trees swayed as if slow music played there, and the tiny hairs on my forearms lifted to the same rhythm.

"Wick?" Mom said in a high-pitched voice, one that I knew very well. When I was nine, I got my fingers caught in the mixer. I had to get stitches. Mom talked to me in that voice all the way to the hospital.

We met Daddy halfway across the yard. He told us Collin had not been arrested because the sheriff knew all of these boys and their families. "The sheriff said, 'Boys will be boys,' " Daddy told us.

"Where is Collin?" Mom asked. His dog, Caboose, regarded us with his tongue curled under at the front teeth like a wad of pink bubble gum. A sure sign he thought Collin was in for trouble.

Me, I was trying to figure out if this was good news or bad, for my party.

"Long gone before I got there," Daddy said, disgusted. "He's out riding around with his draft card–burning friends and the Buford kid." He looked at me. "Did you do what I told you to do?"

My stomach took a sudden fall. Daddy wanted an answer and Mom was waiting to hear what it would be. "Daddy, I can't stop a party the day before it's supposed to happen," I said. "Nobody does that. I'll be a social outcast."

"Get it done inside half an hour, or I will ground you till you are old and gray," Daddy said.

I spun away from them both and started to cry. I hated Collin. Why did he have to be my brother?

"Don't take this out on her," Mom said.

I started to hope that she would stick up for my party. But only for a second. Because Daddy said, "Bobby Buford was behind this, can you believe that?" and my birthday party was forgotten.

Daddy said, "It used to be, when a boy came home a hero, he knew how to behave like one."

"They're young and foolish, Wick," Mom said. "Just boys," she said, like nothing they did could matter. "You know how that is."

I stopped crying and watched them like they were bouncing a ping-pong ball back and forth.

"I didn't have time to be foolish," Daddy said. "There was a war on when *I* was young, and I knew my duty."

Mom said, "Our son's life is what matters. I don't care—"

"I care about whether I can hold my head up in this town," Daddy said. "If Collin is a coward, then he's no son of mine."

In a voice that could have clipped grass, Mom said, "If Collin were really your son, it wouldn't be so easy for you to say that."

My breath caught. Mom *never* reminded any of us that my daddy was Collin's stepfather. It was only Collin who ever brought it up, when he and Daddy didn't agree.

"I fought in the Korean War too," Daddy said, pointing at Mom.

They walked away from each other to cool off. Mom headed for the house, Daddy for his workshop in the garage. They could argue this again later. Much later. After my party.

I hoped Collin's name would still be mud, of course.

3 ALL A MATTER OF OPINION

At first I thought this card-burning business was just business as usual. I acted like I didn't have to make the calls, and Mom didn't mention them. I figured if Collin got home pretty soon, there'd be the big fight and then the storm would blow over. My party still had a chance.

Mom set ten pounds of potatoes to the boil. Steam thickened the air until we could hardly breathe, but Mom chopped onions like she was hammering nails, hard. Her hair coiled like wire in the humidity. She had wedged the electric fan in the open window to take some of the heat out of the kitchen.

My clothes stuck to me anyway.

I usually liked to sit in the rocker near the stove, but the stove got too hot to stay there. Still, I hung around the kitchen, in very little danger of being put to work. Since that time with the mixer blades, Mom didn't trust me with anything more dangerous than a butter knife.

Caboose had taken up a position outside the back door, showing us his "good dog" sit, and he did not scratch at the screen. "Don't let him in," Mom said, even though Caboose sat and sat. When he did slink away, it was because Daddy was about to come in through the back door.

He said to me, "Did you make those calls?" and went upstairs without waiting for an answer.

Mom stabbed the potatoes with a long fork to make sure they were done. I said, "You don't have to kill them. They're already dead."

I got the look of, Jokes will not be appreciated.

As she cooked, I went along behind, cleaning up after her. I waited till she was furiously stirring together condensed milk and mayonnaise to make salad dressing. "You don't have to act like you're mad at me," I said. "This is Collin's fault."

"I know this is hard for you," Mom said, letting the spoon fall still. "But your daddy is right. This is not a good time to have a party."

"Collin's had all summer to burn his draft card," I said, "but no, he had to pick today to do this."

Mom put her hands on her hips. "Are you suggesting he did this to ruin your party?"

"No," I said, because I could see she was getting mad. I put away the celery seed and the dry mustard. Good girl, me. "But I would have felt sorrier for him if he had waited for the day after."

She stared at me for a moment, then went back to stirring. "I have to keep reminding myself this is normal," she said. "You and Collin are going through a stage. It happens to be a time when I am already on the verge of tearing out my hair, but it is only a stage."

"A stage?" I said, amazed. "You think the way Collin ignores me is a stage?"

"It's partly your fault. You do things you know will annoy him."

"You're wrong," I said. "Collin doesn't even know I'm here."

"You and Collin don't think you're close," she said. "As you get older, age makes less and less difference. You'll see."

"Don't tell me," I said. "Tell Collin." When I was little, I tried to follow him like a puppy. He always had someplace he wanted to go, and in my mind's eye, he wore a baseball glove. He never looked back.

My feelings hurt, just remembering that.

"He knows," Mom said. "Your brother cares about you more than you think."

Tears came to my eyes so suddenly, I had to turn away. It was probably the smell of onions in the air or something. Onion odor can make your chest cramp right up, like your heart is breaking, that's what I decided.

Like she thought I was going soft, Mom said, "When your daddy and I pass on to our reward, Collin will be the closest family you have left."

"Low blow," I said, and wiped my eyes. She wasn't the kind of person who used words like *pass on to their reward*. She usually just said someone died.

"I want you to think about how important it is to hold a family together," she said. "How hard life can be without family to help you."

"Family promises birthday parties and then takes them away," I said.

Mom pushed the salad dressing at me. "Stir," she said, "till your arms fall off."

While I stirred, I wished Daddy had gone out there and found Collin in handcuffs. I imagined Mom and Daddy and me driving along the highway and seeing Collin at the side of the road, in stripes and an ankle chain, picking up trash. Like I was waft-ing by on a parade float, I'd wave to sweaty old him as we passed, riding in our air-conditioned sedan. We didn't have an air-conditioned car, so this would really be a dream come true.

From where I stood at the table, I saw when Mrs. Miller crossed the alley and let herself into our backyard. She left the gate hanging open and came through the grass with mincing steps.

I didn't say a word of warning to Mom.

When Mrs. Miller rapped on the screen door, Mom jumped with the shock of it and stepped over to see who was there. She said, "Why—"

"I want you to know I am not a bit surprised," Mrs. Miller said, her tiny eyes gleaming. "I've always known Collin had a bad-boy side."

I perked right up. Mrs. Miller was singing my song. I made a resolution to say something genuinely nice about her to some-body.

Surely it could be done.

Mrs. Miller drew breath to say more, but Mom slammed the inside door. She pulled the curtains on the very sight of the rounded O of Mrs. Miller's mouth.

"She makes you want to hit her," Mom said, looking like she didn't know whether to laugh or cry.

"Not me," I said.

4 SPLIT DOWN THE MIDDLE

Not long after that, Daddy came downstairs and set some things on the porch. I set the salad dressing aside. Daddy went back upstairs and I scooted down the hall for a look outside.

I saw a rolled-up blanket and a pair of work boots. Collin's book bag was stuffed so full of T-shirts that it couldn't be zippered shut. I couldn't believe my eyes. I thought Daddy was just talking mad when he said Collin was no son of his.

Family photographs were hanging all up and down that wall along the stairs, and Daddy knocked them all a-kilter, coming down with another armload of stuff. He looked as determined as I had ever seen. I watched him perch Collin's baseball glove right on top of the pile.

I was already sweating from the heat in the kitchen, but a new sweat broke over that and I shivered. When Daddy brushed past me to come back inside, I went back to the kitchen and told Mom what he was up to.

I asked her, "Is he kidding?"

Her face had gone as white as the salad dressing. "Does he look like he's in the mood to be funny?"

"I mean, he's bluffing. Right?" It had never occurred to me

that one of us could do something so wrong, Daddy would flat-out lock the door against us.

"I'm going to make a sheet of zucchini bread," Mom said. She told me to go out to the backyard to pick zucchinis. "Everything over the size of a banana," she said, measuring flour into a great big mixing bowl.

I could see she'd already used up her entire set of Rubbermaid refrigerator dishes to store the potato salad. I hoped she didn't expect us to eat through zucchini bread for twenty people as well.

"Are we going to a funeral I don't know about?" I asked.

"Go."

"I have cleaned this house from top to bottom," I yelled. Caboose slipped inside as I opened the screen door. I didn't try to stop him. "You should be making me a birthday cake."

I slammed the door behind me.

I rummaged through the garden, angrily twisting off zucchinis. All those prickly hairs on the leaves made my arms itch something fierce. I knew I'd been sent out there so Mom could tell Daddy he was acting like a crazy person.

I wanted to shout, My father has gone nuts, and my mom is not far behind. But I didn't. My mouth felt too dry.

One of our neighbors came out to take her sheets off the clothesline. I had been babysitting for her all summer. When she waved to me, I felt like she was waving from a faraway place where I used to live.

I couldn't wave back.

I went back into the kitchen, carrying what could have passed for an armload of green baseball bats. Caboose was sitting under the table, his head hanging low. Mom said, "Make your calls."

"Noooo."

"Call," she said in a deep choked voice. Mom hardly ever cried. I knew how to deal with mad, but not sad. All the fight drained right out of me. I spent the next hour uninviting all the kids I had asked over.

I was so embarrassed. The boys sounded like they'd been let loose from a foot trap. All except my cousin Theo, who was out at the farm. Uncle Buck said he thought Theo had forgotten about the party anyway.

The girls were not as nice about it as they could have been. Especially the ones who loaned me their records. Especially when I said I couldn't bring them back right that minute.

Except for my cousin Dolly, who hadn't loaned me any records. She lived out about forty miles away, near my grandma's farm. She wouldn't have known most of the kids I'd invited. She said, "Don't worry about it. I bet the boys weren't going to dance anyway."

So I'd lost my last chance for a party. Besides my cousins, I figured my friend Judy—who had not yet come home from visiting her aunt in Chicago, so she didn't yet know my party was off—was the only friend I had left.

"Thank you, Collin," I said out loud. His dog's ears perked up at the sound of Collin's name. "Thank you very much." But deep inside, I had begun to worry about my brother, just a little. I wondered what he'd do if—I tried to ignore the part that came after *if*.

After the zucchini bread went into the oven, Mom went into the living room to talk to Daddy. "I wish you would be reasonable," Mom said to him. "We could just send Collin on out to the farm while we sort things out."

"Where else would he go?" Daddy said, like another thought had never entered his mind.

I said, "You want Collin to go out to Grandma's?"

"Grace—" Daddy pointed his finger.

I didn't know which way to turn anymore. I had been feeling almost sorry for Collin. But this was more than I could take. I said, "That's like saying, 'Ooh, you're punished, you bad boy. Eat these hot biscuits with grape jelly, and I hope you're sorry now.' "

Mom turned me around and headed me back to the kitchen, which was her way of saying that I had better not say another word. She didn't fool me one bit. She didn't want Daddy to change his mind.

She started in on frying chicken. She had worked herself down to the last egg, the flour bin was empty, and the chicken parts were running low. I did not lift a finger to help. Now that my birthday party was being talked about for all the wrong reasons, I could devote my full attention to being mad. I waited for Mom to ask me to do another thing.

She didn't.

After a while, the good smells in the kitchen worked their magic. I had not forgotten I was mad, but I had remembered it wasn't Mom's fault. I sat parked at the table, nibbling on warm zucchini bread.

When I heard the doorknob rattle, I leaned my chair back on two legs to get a clear view. Collin's dog was split down the middle with wanting to go to the door and wanting to be next to fried chicken.

I didn't doubt Collin had noticed his bedroll on the porch. But I thought he might not get it right off, that the welcome mat had been yanked inside. Collin tried to open the door and then he knocked.

Daddy had been sitting in the front room watching demolition derbies on the TV for at least two hours. He looked to be mindless as a Big Boy tomato. He didn't move.

Ever since Collin printed STOP THE WAR in red paint that dripped down the back of his jacket, the going had been rough between my brother and my daddy. But getting into trouble at our house used to mean getting yelled at. Getting grounded. I didn't know what to make of it when Daddy put our stuff on the porch.

"Mom," I said. I thought maybe she didn't hear Collin, what with the noise of the fan, and she was scraping fried bits off the bottom of the pan.

Collin looked into the front room window, saw Daddy, and yelled, "Hey." That did it for the dog. He trotted off to stand at the locked front door, his whole hind end a-wagging, expecting any second Collin would walk in.

I said, "Mom? Collin's out front."

She went out the back door, the spatula still in her hand. After a minute I went into the front room and stood where I could see out the window. In that kind of afternoon light that makes me think of movies with happy endings, Mom put her arms around Collin. The greasy spatula left a print on the back of his shirt.

When they let go of each other, Collin made a slow, thoughtful movement of pushing his cap to the back of his head. It was a gesture so like Daddy's own that I wanted him to see it. "Look."

Daddy didn't act like he'd heard me.

"Look!" I said, but then it was over.

Caboose barked, one bark, asking to go out. Collin looked back at the house, squinting against the sunlight. I knew he could not see into this room. But I felt as if he looked right at me before he walked away.

5 SORRY WON'T HELP

When Mom came back in, she turned over the frying pieces of chicken before she did anything else. I could tell she was still worked up over the good-byes. I waited, one foot jiggling.

Then she told me Collin would spend the night at one of his friends' houses. Mom said it in the tone of, Until things calm down around here. I didn't like the picture this brought to mind at all, even if I was the one who didn't want him to go out to Grandma's.

Collin would hate having to ask his friends. I could faster see him sleeping under the bleachers at the ball field. Mom made it sound like all we had to do was wait for Daddy to come to his senses. The way I saw it, I was going to have to wait for everybody to come to their senses, and it was likely to be a long wait.

"Your brother said to tell you he's sorry about your party," Mom said. She looked like she figured the next thing would be, I'd bust a spring. I surprised her. I went to my room without saying one word.

I was still mad at Collin, but I couldn't help wondering if he was standing on the corner hoping Daddy would change his mind. Besides, I didn't blame him for my party as much as I blamed Mom. She could have put her foot down and said my party was going to go on anyway.

But most of my mad settled itself on Daddy, and that surprised me.

It had been bothering me all afternoon, the way he sat there watching TV, like what he did shouldn't be argued by anybody. I got to thinking back to the day my cousin Theo's older brother was supposed to graduate.

Thatcher had been named class valedictorian, so nearly the whole fam-dam-ily had showed up to see it. Everybody had showed up except Thatcher. It didn't take ten minutes for word to get around that he had likely headed for Canada the night before.

I got the feeling some people—my aunts and Grandma, to name a few—breathed a sigh of relief when they heard Thatcher had hit the road. So it took a little longer for me to get it that some other people were upset about it. Once I figured that part out, mostly I just felt sorry for my uncle.

He kept apologizing to everyone at the ceremony, even to people who hadn't come to see Thatcher, but to see their own kids graduate. It wasn't his fault Thatcher didn't show up to give the valedictorian speech. A lot of people probably felt sorry for him, even if they were mad at Thatcher.

This was not the same thing at all.

I didn't see why Daddy got to sit around behaving like it was his own personal tragedy that Collin burned his draft card. I'd lost out on my party, and Mom didn't look too happy either. This was our family house, of course, but once I started thinking about it, I remembered it was also Mom and Collin's house before she married Daddy.

It was still hers, he was always proud to say Mom had paid off the house by painting furniture. It was Daddy's fault, and only Daddy's fault, that Collin couldn't come in Mom's house.

I blamed Collin for everything but that.

Supper was fried chicken and potato salad, needless to say. This was usually greeted with more enthusiasm. Mom and I ate first, then Daddy came to eat while we washed dishes. He didn't have a thing to say, not even when Mom tore the meat off a big piece of chicken and fed it to the dog.

When Mom came into my room at bedtime, I asked her, "Doesn't Daddy love Collin anymore?"

"Of course he does," Mom said, coming back to sit on my bed.

"He threw him out," I said.

"He'll be sorry he did that," Mom said, "once he gets over being mad."

"Sometimes people do something so wrong that sorry doesn't help," I said. "I've heard Daddy say that."

Tears came to a shine in Mom's eyes. She said, "You could ask Judy over to supper for your birthday tomorrow."

"Thanks, but no thanks." Even though my heart did lift a little.

Hope must be made of really tough stuff if it was still able to draw breath around here, that's all I could say.

6 SUPPER TABLE BLUES

The next morning the family pictures had all been straightened on the wall. Daddy made blueberry pancakes, which was his way of making peace.

Mom ate zucchini bread. There was no talking at the table. There were a lot of pancakes going cold. I had a little of each, pancakes and zucchini bread. I went back to bed feeling sick to my stomach.

Caboose followed me, and he didn't look like a happy dog.

Mom went out to work in the garden. That's where she found out that Collin had gone to stay with his girlfriend's family. She came back into the house and shouted that she wanted a lock put on that back gate. She wanted barbed wire laid over the top of the fence.

I went downstairs to find out what was going on. Daddy was not in front of the TV anymore. "It wouldn't hurt to get a big mean dog either," I heard Mom say. I went into the kitchen.

She was cleaning her fingernails with a hard little brush, saying to Daddy, "Mrs. Miller came right up to me like she was my nearest sister." It made me cringe, the way Mom scrubbed her fingernails. "She told me Collin has taken up with big-city trash."

"Then what?" Daddy said.

"I lobbed a tomato at her," Mom said. "It was there on the ground, soft and slug-chewed, and before I thought better of it, that tomato was in the air."

I didn't say one word. I knew better.

Daddy said, "Most times that woman is so wrong, she could be taken for a left turn."

Mom took this for a don't-worry and dropped that nailbrush with a sigh of relief. I realized I'd started holding my breath. I made myself relax a little.

Then Daddy added, "Just our luck to be on her right-hand side." He slammed a fist against the wall and said, "I can't believe he spent the night at Kerrie's."

Me either. But we should have guessed. Her parents, both of them, taught at the college. They had that basement playroom where kids stayed over sometimes. Boys and girls both.

This was not good news. Daddy had never taken to Kerrie. She wore low jeans that let her belly button show, and she tied a bandanna over her head like a migrant worker. She said words like *trippy* when she liked something a whole lot.

Back when Collin saw fit to put holes in the knees of brand-new jeans and took to wearing a peace sign for a necklace, Kerrie got the blame. Collin got in trouble, but Kerrie got the blame.

I figured staying at Kerrie's was Collin's way of getting back at Daddy. Not that I could say so. Mom thought Collin was stamped *good boy* at birth. She didn't want to hear it from me that he could be spiteful.

From the look on Daddy's face, I guessed he wasn't saying so either.

I went back to my room and didn't talk to anyone but Caboose the whole day long. I did see Judy crossing her lawn when she came home from the airport. Something weird and awful had been done to her hair. It would have been great fun to tell her the whole sad saga of my party, only she didn't call.

I got closer to a birthday than I expected. I thought I had completely lost the mood for it, but the mood came back a little bit when I found two tiny presents next to my plate at suppertime.

The presents were wrapped up in the jewelry store paper, so I knew they would be charms for my bracelet. I knew which ones I wanted, and I'd made sure Mom knew which ones too.

She had poked candles into a slab of the zucchini bread. It was a long way from the party I had hoped for. Not even my cousins would be there to cheer me on as I made a wish.

I didn't say a word about it. We were all too shivery and fragile after the first night and day of Collin doesn't live here anymore. There were cards to be opened, with money from relatives.

Mom told me to go ahead and open the presents. The first charm turned out to be a teeny tiny birthday cake with candles, and the next one was the word *party!* Just like that, with punctuation.

I could hardly believe my eyes. A birthday cake? Party?

The cruelty.

Mom said, "I'm sorry, Grace. I asked Collin to pick up those charms for me a month ago. He let the store wrap them up and I never got to see them."

"Thank you," I said, "for making this birthday so special."

"That's no way to talk to your mother," Daddy said.

We all looked at each other in our varying ways, no one happy with anybody else. Mom and Daddy declared a truce long enough to talk about nothing over supper but what ought to be done about Collin's situation. Mrs. Miller had called it a criminal offense. Mom and Daddy called it his *situation*.

Daddy said, "He's good with machinery. The army will probably put him to work in a repair shop. He'll be out of harm's way."

Mom said, "He's going to be drafted any day now. We have to talk about what we can do for him, surely you can see that."

Daddy said, "Collin needs this. The army turns boys into confident men."

Mom said, "The army gives boys permission to do things they've been forbidden to do their whole lives up to that point, like shoot at people."

Daddy ate like he had a room to fill, but Mom had forgotten she held a forkful of potato salad in midair. She kept on holding it there.

I had not yet forgiven Collin for ruining my birthday, but I had begun to realize that if I were facing something I really didn't want to do, I would rather have Mom arguing for me than Daddy.

"The next time Cronkite tallies up how many of our boys have died over there, I want you to pay attention." Walter Cronkite told us the war news on TV every night. Daddy wanted to make some reply to this, but Mom had gotten up a fair head of steam.

"Collin still has a chance," Mom said. "Boys who come home unable to dress themselves or walk the dog don't have another chance. Their parents can be feeding a grown man like a baby and taking him to the bathroom, and wondering who will do that for him when they're too old, or have died. Is that what you want for us?"

Daddy held up a piece of mail. "This conversation isn't about what we want. He's supposed to show up for duty."

Mom looked shaken. "His draft notice?"

"I guess you ought to call over there and tell him," Daddy said.

"This doesn't settle anything," Mom said, but I could see her resolve had taken a beating.

"It's time for Collin to grow up and be a man," Daddy said, standing up to leave the table.

"I want him to live long enough to be one," Mom said, dropping her fork on the plate.

I was the only one left at the table after that.

The candles had not been lit.

Happy birthday to me.

7 SMALL MYSTERIES

Mom walked around after supper with a set to her face, like she had more to say. The way Caboose walks around with a ball in his mouth, waiting for someone to play. Only Mom wasn't in the mood to play. Daddy got into his truck and drove off. He didn't tell us where he was going.

Although I never heard her say it in so many words, Mom seemed to think Daddy was partly to blame for the war because he was a man and because he'd been to war. He never made his war sound like a good thing, but he made it sound like a proud thing.

Daddy never talked about dying either. He never made war sound as bad as what we heard on the news. I never said it to anyone, but what I heard on the news didn't feel true to me.

My grandfather died a few years ago. That didn't feel true at first either. Even after the funeral was over, I thought about him as if he were still alive. I felt like I would see him the next time I went out to the farm. It took a few times of not finding him there for it to sink in.

People died, I knew that. But it was hard to imagine somebody playing softball on Tuesday nights one week, and the next week they were made to get into a helicopter where people would shoot at them like ducks over a lake.

I knew it felt true for Mom because it had happened to Collin's dad. Maybe it scared her more than it did Daddy because, although he had gone to war, he had also come home safely.

When I got up the next morning, I thought maybe it would be a good idea to mention that to Mom.

Right after breakfast.

She was not in the kitchen to fry an egg. She'd left zucchini bread out for me. I poured cereal into a bowl, thinking she must be out in the shed, painting little creatures of the field on the buffet.

This piece of furniture was to be our wedding present to my uncle Milford, who was getting married in the fall. Almost everybody else in the family was working together on building a house for Uncle Milford, but my mom liked to do things on her own. Marching to a different drummer, she called it.

After I ate, I went out to the shed to see how the painting was coming along. That's when I knew that Mom was not home at all. I went back to the kitchen. She had not left a note. I hung around on the porch swing, waiting, and then I roamed the house when it got too hot outside.

Mom didn't come back until noon. She went right to her painting. I watched her mix colors with thinner. "I was starting to wonder if I should call Daddy," I told her.

"Did you?" she said. "Call him?"

"No."

"You and your daddy aren't having an easy time, I know," Mom said. "It would be better for both of you if you didn't take it out on each other."

"Me? Whose birthday party did I cancel?" I asked her. "Whose brother did I throw out of the house?"

Mom's mouth twitched like she wanted to smile.

This bothered me. "What?"

She said, "Did I hear you say you wish Collin was here?"

I hadn't put it quite that way, but each of us, for our own reasons, did want Collin to be where he was supposed to be. I said, "What's so funny about that?"

Mom was not around for breakfast again the next day. Once I was sure I had the house to myself, I went up to Collin's bedroom to nose around. It hit me that something was different in Collin's room. Something besides his not being there.

I glanced around, but I couldn't decide what had changed. I spotted this paperback book with a picture of what looked to me like Indian feathers on the front. Collin had been carrying it around in his hip pocket for months.

When I picked it up off his desk and read the title, *Johnny Got His Gun*, I realized it showed two fingers, held up in the peace sign. I shoved the book into the pocket of my robe. I liked the feel of it there, and I kept it.

I was downstairs when Mom came home, bringing in only half a bag of groceries to show for her time. "You don't fool me one bit," I said. "I know where you've been."

Even though, until I saw the look on her face, I hadn't been sure. "Grace, all of this is going to make more sense when you're older," Mom said.

I doubted it.

Mom made another secret trip to see Collin the next morning. Me, I went back to his room to snoop. I couldn't help myself.

I took his red cap, with Lonnie's Auto Repair Service written on it in hard white thread. Collin wore this cap only to fix cars at Lonnie's. It did not have one black oily spot on it. Collin loved working at Lonnie's.

I shoved the cap into the dusty space under my dresser. I wasn't sure why I didn't put it back in his room. It wasn't like I could wear it around. I didn't even want to.

When the morning wore on and Mom didn't come home, I went through his drawers. Mostly they were too neat to belong to a normal kid. But in a bottom drawer, under some more books, I spotted a flier with a heading that said, "What's Vietnam Like?"

I read it and learned these two men had come to the high school to talk to the kids. To the boys. It didn't sound like they were much in favor of going to war.

Under that I found a magazine folded open to an article with pictures of what looked like a long wall of black plastic bags stacked up next to a plane. I read that that was how they sent dead soldiers home, in those bags. Disgusting. Sad too.

Between the pages of the magazine were torn-out and folded-up pieces of newspaper, all of them stories having to do with the war. I wanted to read them too, but I heard a noise in the house. I shoved them back in the drawer and skedaddled, my heart beating too fast.

8 FAMILY SECRETS

Caboose came up the stairs while I was trying to look like I'd been in my room all along. It took me a minute to realize that I was still alone. I'd only heard the dog rattling his food dish around.

I went back to Collin's room and looked around some more. Something *was* different, but I couldn't put my finger on it.

Then I heard a screen door slam, and I beat it back to my room again. Mom came upstairs and stopped for a moment before she went on down the hall. I caught only a glimpse of her out of the corner of my eye because I was so busy rearranging the stuffed animals on my bed.

Neither of us said a word about what we'd been up to.

Only a few minutes later, Grandma's big Dodge wallowed to a stop by the back door, stuffed to the seams. Aunt Birdie leaned out the front passenger window. Grandma didn't go anywhere without her.

We were all real tender toward Aunt Birdie and her little girl, Stellie, since Uncle Sawyer had gone missing. We loved them before, of course, only now we made sure to show it. It was easy to include Aunt Birdie all the time, because she was so tiny, she could sit on somebody's lap like a child.

Everybody poured out of that car and piled up on the porch, seven of my aunts and Grandma, all dressed Sunday-go-to-meeting. Grandma always dressed up to view Mom's wedding presents. "We've come to see how your painting is coming along," Grandma said.

"Helen, I'm so sorry," Mom said, her face bright as she opened the door to them. "I forgot you were coming by today. Oh, I feel so thoughtless."

"If you have a glass of sweet tea in the house, you're forgiven," Grandma said cheerily. "Surely that buffet hasn't taken a walk. We can still look."

"It's in the shed," Mom said, smiling in that way that always brought out her lilting hostess voice. "Grace, why don't you take everyone out to see it? Be sure to tell them I work on it night and day, now, won't you?"

This was only the fourth painted wedding present, but it seemed like one of my uncles got married every year. There were so many of them. Seventeen on Daddy's side alone.

Grandma called some of the boys her latecomers, because they weren't her boys until they were eight or ten or fourteen years of age. They were boys who, for one reason or another, found themselves destitute and homeless during the Depression. I gathered that also meant they were found by the side of the road.

Most of them were old men now, older than Mom and Daddy. When Grandma came into the house, she went to her favorite seat, the rocker by the stove. I asked her to tell me once more the story about her boys.

"I had three school-age boys and two smaller ones when Pop brought the first child home," she said. "He brought four more boys home over that summer.

"All the boys but the littlest shared a double bed, sleeping crosswise. We fashioned a makeshift dining table from a door and set wooden barrels around it to sit on. At first it was like eating from a raft set with plates."

Grandma rocked back and forth once, then said, "I never bothered to count noses. I gave sleepy faces their chores in the morning, and whoever showed up for supper got tucked in at night."

"Which ones are the latecomers, Grandma?" I asked.

"That's for me to know and you to wonder," she said firmly. "Not that it makes any difference now. One suppertime I looked at all those children sitting around the table as if they had always been together, and thought, This is my family. A raft of boys."

I liked the sound of that. It felt right, like a flock of birds, a herd of cattle. I had this picture come to me, a raft of boys being borne through floodwaters to the safety of Grandma's dining room.

When Grandma went home, she took with her three bowls of potato salad. I was grateful to see that stuff go. Her visit lasted two hours. Collin's name never came up.

9 A BITTER TASTE

Meanwhile, Daddy had plans of his own.

"I'm going over there to talk to Kerrie's folks," he said that evening at supper. "They have to understand. If Collin doesn't show his face where he's supposed to, he's going to be in big trouble."

Mom, who was carrying three glasses, set them down hard at the corner of the table, sloshing sweet tea over the sides. Caboose had been sleeping in the corner of the room, but he slunk off like he'd heard someone fire a warning shot. I wished I could go with him. Mealtimes meant fighting times these days.

"What are you going to say?" Mom said.

Daddy said, "They can't go on encouraging him to ignore his responsibilities."

"You don't know what they're telling him," Mom said. "They gave him a bed and a place at the table, and so far as you know, that's all."

"Just one look at that daughter of theirs tells me all I need to know about their politics," Daddy said.

"Their daughter is not my business," Mom said. "I've talked to them. It isn't their politics that opened their door, but the kindness of their hearts. If you gave it some thought, you might remember that people with open doors usually have open minds."

Daddy said, "You're talking like one of those hippies."

"Maybe I am," Mom said, like she was glad to hear it.

She went back to the kitchen without saying another word. So I was the one who heard Daddy say, under his breath, "If they hadn't taken him in, we'd have settled this by now."

I never meant to speak up. Words just fell out of my mouth. "You shouldn't have thrown him out."

Daddy flinched, knocking over the tea glass he'd set in front of me. He rushed to mop up the table with paper napkins, saying, "No one asked you for your opinion, Grace."

I stood up. "Family takes people in, it doesn't throw them out." I was so mad that spit flew out of my mouth.

Daddy said, "It's not too late for you to get a taste of the same medicine—"

"Sit down, Grace," Mom said, coming back with two plates of spaghetti and meatballs. She narrowed her eyes at Daddy. "Or are you going to throw her out too?"

I sat. I was shaking all over.

"This whole family is getting out of hand," Daddy said, taking fork in one hand and knife in the other. He set the heels of his fists on the table, caveman style. "I don't want to hear any more about who's right and who's wrong. I am the head of this family and what I say goes, *goes*."

"You're the boss," Mom said in a flat tone that should have been warning enough, even for Daddy.

"That's right," he said. "Now give me my supper."

Mom flipped the plates so the spaghetti landed right in his lap.

I screamed a little. I didn't mean to, but I did. Meatballs rolled across the floor. All but for one that hit the table with a wet thump. Daddy looked like a big hand had reached down, tipped him over and shaken him hard. He looked that shocked.

He took a plate from Mom and scraped everything he could back onto it, which wasn't much. Most of the spaghetti had slithered to the floor. He wiped his hand on his pants and went upstairs.

Mom and I got down on the floor to pick up the rest of the mess. The spaghetti kept sliding away, like it did when Daddy tried to catch it, but it was worse because our hands were shaking so bad. It wasn't really funny, but we started to get the giggles, and for about half a minute it seemed hilarious.

"This isn't funny," Mom said. "Our nerves are shot."

When I stood up, I spotted the meatball that rested near my plate and popped the whole thing into my mouth. In my opinion, Collin's dog was about to eat real well. I had just swallowed when I noticed Mom looking at me like I was something that had crawled out of a dark place.

I said, "It's nerves." But it was no good. I knew the way my mom thought, and in her opinion, if I really felt Collin had been wronged, that meatball should have left a bitter taste in my mouth.

One thing was crystal clear. I was not going to be invited to sit in the empty chair marked "favorite" now that Collin was made to move out.

10 FROM BAD TO WORSE

Daddy didn't come home for dinner the next night. "He's eating at Wally's greasy spoon," Mom said.

We had grilled cheese sandwiches on the porch swing.

"He is the stubbornest man alive," she said, ignoring her sandwich. "Stubborn grows on his family tree. It's a trait they pass down like freckles and sandy hair."

"Collin's pretty stubborn," I said, giving a kick to start the swing. We were all of us, in this household, stubborn. If there was another way to be, nobody ever told me.

"Collin's hot-headed, that's all," Mom told me. "I don't know where he gets that from. His daddy never gave me a bit of trouble."

Every so often over the next couple of days, I would catch a glimpse of Collin's hat, still right where I stuck it under my dresser. It made me feel spiteful and small, but I didn't retrieve it. After a while I wouldn't look there anymore.

At mealtimes, Mom talked like she'd unlocked a Pandora's box of things unsaid from years back. She told me she didn't know when my daddy had become so narrow-minded. She didn't know why she didn't see it in him before.

She told me how much more like his own daddy Collin had

turned out to be, and she was glad of it—she didn't want to raise bullheaded children. She finished this off with a meaningful glance in my direction.

I could see things going from bad to worse before my very own eyes. I thought it was time for someone to tell Daddy to come on home to supper. After Mom went to bed, taking Caboose with her, I sneaked back to the living room to wait. I woke up hearing Daddy come in. I followed him up the stairs in time to see him go into Collin's room.

I halted on the stairs, wondering if this meant that Daddy was on the verge of letting Collin come home, but it felt wrong all over. When Daddy came out into the hallway a minute later, his bare feet gleamed white in the glow of the night-light.

And then I got it—the something different in Collin's room. It was the faint scent of Old Spice. I'd noticed it, but I hadn't wondered why I could smell Daddy's cologne in Collin's room.

I knew why now. He was sleeping in there.

I felt weak and sweaty, like I could vomit.

I sank back into the shadows until Daddy went into the bathroom. Then I ran to my bed and dragged the bedspread up to my chin. For a long time I lay shivering in the darkness.

In the week that followed, things looked much the same on the surface. Daddy started coming home to supper. Mom didn't dump anything in his lap. They talked to each other in such a careful way that I started to wish they would fight it out.

On top of this, we endured terrible hot winds. The only relief came as sudden brief periods of silence when the air quit moving, such complete stillness that the sweat on our skin wouldn't drip.

Then it rained hard. Thunder boomed, and lightning danced

through the wet streets. The wind blew the way we were used to. Still, things didn't feel right to me. I started testing the changes around our house.

I could eat in the front room. I could play records as loud as I wanted. Even the dog knew things were different. Caboose started sleeping on the couch. Neither Mom nor Daddy noticed.

Mom never sat still. When the painting was done, she worked in the garden till she was tired enough to fall asleep when she sat down. During a rainstorm she went through the house, cleaning things that had not seen light in years.

Every so often Mom looked surprised to see me. When this happened, she asked me two or three times what I had done all day, like she could hardly hear anything I said. Like we were not in the same room.

Sometimes while she was telling me something, she would break off in the middle of a sentence and stare off into space. After a while, I felt like I lived alone.

Collin had always been just out of reach as a brother, and even as a friend. But it sank in, slowly, that once he moved out of Mom's and Daddy's reach as well, it did not draw me closer to the center of us, but pushed me further off to the side.

Then I heard Mom in Collin's room in the middle of the day.

11 Get Me a Suitcase

Wire hangers scraped fast across the closet pole. A dresser drawer slammed shut. I tiptoed along the carpet runner until I stood outside Collin's bedroom. His clothes were piled willy-nilly on the bed, mounds of shirts and underwear, sweaters and a pair of new jeans. The sight stole my breath away.

When Mom looked up, she said, "Get me a suitcase from the attic, Grace. That small brown one. He can't carry much." She sat down on the end of the bed, with an air of I-give-up. "I don't know what to do about his winter coat."

I asked, "Where's he going?"

"Canada."

"He can't do that," I said, my heart starting to pound. "Daddy's going to be rabid."

Mom looked at me the same way she'd looked at me when she told me a car hit our old collie and I asked if she'd let me get a cat. A look made up of a strange mix of love and disappointment, as if she felt she had never managed to do her right work on me.

"Well, he will be," I said. "Rabid. And Collin's 'good boy' reputation is going to go right down the drain, I hope you know."

"I suppose," she said, "you'd rather see Collin wearing a buzz cut and army boots?"

"That's not what I meant."

"I know," Mom said. "But that is Collin's only other choice."

I said exactly the wrong thing. "I bet Daddy hasn't heard a thing about this. Has he?"

Mom's face reddened. "I'll talk this out with him later. Right now, I'm taking these things over to Kerrie's house. Collin's going from there."

I said, "I don't want anything to do with this."

"Then I guess you better go back to your room."

I did, but only after I'd stormed downstairs and up again, punching the wall with the heel of my fist every few steps. It felt good to hear those picture frames rattle, even though my wrists hurt like the dickens.

I yelled from the stairs, "If Collin was so all-fired anxious to go, why didn't he go with Thatcher on graduation day?"

There was no reply, just the sound of a drawer sliding shut. "I hope you know what you're doing," I shouted, and I went into my room. "I just hope you do." I slammed my bedroom door.

A kind of panic built inside me. Where was Collin going to be? Would he have enough to eat? We had never heard a word from Thatcher. My mother would really go crazy if she had to worry about Collin that way.

I didn't want to worry about Collin that way either.

I opened the drawer next to my bed and snatched up my savings. Twenty-five dollars was birthday money. The rest, thirty dollars, was the first money I'd ever made—babysitting for the horrible twins next door. It was all rolled up tight with a blue rubber band.

I heard Mom going up to the attic. I didn't stop to think. I ran down the hallway on tiptoe and stuffed the wad of money deep into the pocket of Collin's folded jeans.

I had no sooner smoothed down the lump it made than I started thinking better of giving it to him. Some of that money was hard-earned. If Mom hadn't started down the attic stairs, I might have snatched it back. But I had to hit it back to my room, lickety-split.

I fell across my bed. My heart was beating so hard. I knew right then that if Daddy found out what I'd done, he'd never love me as much again.

Mom stopped by my door, now standing open. She said, "Last chance to say good-bye."

I didn't answer. I was caught between them, Mom and Daddy.

I knew exactly how much of this trouble could be laid at each person's feet. Collin, Daddy, and Mom. All of it came amazingly clear to me, much the way I felt when I put the last few pieces of a jigsaw puzzle into place.

I purely hated them all.

12 Not Talking to You

When Mom left for Kerrie's, I slammed my door as hard as I could, even though I was the only one there to hear it. Then I made a sign that read NOT TALKING TO YOU, taped it to the outside of my door and slammed it shut again.

I threw myself down on my bed, and while I was lying there, noticed Collin's hat under my dresser. I could hardly believe he wasn't coming back for that hat.

He wasn't going to be working at Lonnie's anymore, and that hat wouldn't mean anything more to him than a fond memory. He wasn't coming back for the stuff Mom left in his drawers, or for the posters on his walls, or his dog.

I suddenly felt like I loved Caboose more than anybody else in the world. When he scratched at my door and whined, I opened it and let him in. I cried into his fur. I promised to love him so much, he wouldn't miss Collin. He wouldn't even know Collin was gone.

I would never have left that sign there for Mom to see. Between making Caboose feel better and then trying to figure out what I'd tell Daddy when he found out my savings were gone, I got sidetracked. For a minute I thought there was nothing worse than putting my money in Collin's pants that were going to Canada.

Excuse-wise, I came up with, He's my brother, and he shopped for my birthday presents. Neither of which seemed like good enough reasons, even to me. But I knew I would give Collin the money again.

I just didn't want Daddy to be mad that I did.

I stopped looking for excuses, and thought about what that money could mean to Collin. He had to have money to eat—I couldn't bear to think of him going hungry. Which should have been reason enough for anybody, but I didn't think it was going to be reason enough for Daddy.

He'd said he would not be able to stand tall in this town once Collin was known to be a draft dodger. And he would feel like I was siding against him. I couldn't think of a reason that he'd agree with.

So I was still sitting on the floor with my arms wrapped around Caboose when I heard Mom coming up the stairs. She stopped in front of my door for a moment, then shut herself up in the bathroom to cry.

I really never meant to make her feel worse. I didn't think she'd come back so quick.

I tore that sign down and went outside to sit on the porch swing. The soft sway of it started to bother me, so I moved to the steps. It was too hot, the kind of heat that foretells a storm.

Dandelions had popped up in the lawns all around ours, looking cheerful about rain on the way. Daddy had kept our grass mowed down to the roots since Collin had gone, and bald patches had started to form. A dandelion didn't stand a fighting chance in our yard.

Judy, from next door, found me sitting on the steps in a deep blue funk. She'd called three times, but it was never a time when I could talk about what was going on around my house. She only wanted to talk about her trip anyway. And her beehive hairdo, that's what she called it. She had her own Max Factor lipstick in the cutest oval purple box. When she opened it, the lipstick popped up.

We moved to the swing.

I wanted Judy to sit with me, despite not only my own sorry state but, to be truthful, hers. She had teased the front of her hair up high and combed it smooth, then hair-sprayed the whole mess into paralysis. The back of her head, where she hadn't combed over the teasing, looked like her hair had been fried. For a little while I could pretend my family was not what they said on the news, a war-torn country.

"Just like in the magazines, isn't it?" she said, admiring herself in the little lipstick mirror. "You ought to let me do yours the same way."

"Thanks, but not now," I said. "Maybe when the weather cools off." Maybe when the Sahara freezes over and the camels start ice-skating from one mirage to the next, I said to myself. I felt a little ragtag sitting there next to Judy in my old shorts, her in a pretty sundress, but I did not feel stupid.

I did try her lipstick, though. "It's your color," she said. "Poppy pink." Whenever Judy came back from a visit with her aunt, it took two or three days for her to get back to sounding like a normal human being.

She dabbed some makeup over a bruise on my shin. She said,

"Have you started to think about school clothes? Short skirts are all the fashion." She told me I should never wear short skirts with knee socks. "Tights," she said. "They'll hide all the scars on your knees."

Three tiny scars she was talking about. I pulled away, saying, "I'm not hiding my knees."

Judy finally noticed my gloom. "Heard your birthday party was called off. What happened?"

I said, "Collin went to a sit-in. Now everybody's mad at everybody else." I wanted to tell her more, but I couldn't bring myself to do it. I didn't need Daddy's warning not to tell. Now that Collin had done more than move out, something about this whole mess felt too private to share.

"A sit-in, huh?" The corners of Judy's mouth quirked up. "I suppose the next thing will be he gets on the thumb train to Canada?"

At first this remark didn't sit right with me. But then I shrugged and said, "Boys will be boys."

Mom heard everything through the open window. She pushed the screen door open so fast, it slammed against the house. Her hair stood away from her face like the bride of Frankenstein. Her eyes were just as wide.

We stood up off the swing with the shock of it. It would've been funny if we weren't so scared. Poor Judy was breathing with her mouth open, like a cornered animal.

"I want you inside, Grace," Mom shouted. She stopped at that, to get hold of herself. She sounded almost normal when she said, "Good to see you home, Judy. Surely your mother must have missed you."

Judy took the hint. As she ran across the street, her hair

didn't bounce when she did. It looked like a helmet, it was so entirely controlled. Then I turned on my mother. "You didn't have to do that."

"Come inside," Mom said. "We'll talk."

"I'm not talking to you." This time I meant it.

13 ON THE RUN

Later that day, the only thing on my mind was my money. Every few weeks Daddy would say to me, "Bring out your hoard" so we could gloat over it together. I figured we were due for one of those sessions soon, since I'd gotten the birthday money.

I hadn't yet figured out how to explain myself to Daddy when there was a knock at the front door. A man called, "Anybody home?" through the screen.

"Milford!" Mom called from the kitchen. "I'm back here." Uncle Milford had one leg shorter than the other, so he had an odd gait. I only had to hear him walk to know when it was him. It kept him from being drafted, which for once made a limp seem like a good thing.

I wanted to go downstairs to say hello, but things were so awkward between Mom and me, I was embarrassed. So I crept to the top of the stairs as Uncle Milford went on to the kitchen.

He was the one getting married. Last summer, Uncle Milford taught my cousin Dolly and me to drive. It still made me grin to think of us sitting high on a pile of feed store catalogs, weaving back and forth across the road. Turning the radio up loud. Bobbing our heads to the music. Finally, singing at the tops of our lungs.

We came close to putting Uncle Milford's truck in the ditch more than once. He called us lunatics. He said we made a nervous wreck of him. He still taught us. Our cousin Theo's big brother had taught him, and Uncle Milford made it his business to teach Dolly and me.

I slid down the stairs a little ways, wanting to hear what else they said. Uncle Milford said they needed Collin out to Grandma's farm. Mom made some excuse about the auto repair business being real busy lately. She practically made it sound like Collin owned Lonnie's Auto Repair.

I heard Mom go right to teasing him about the wedding, saying, "I hope you got your fill of being a free man. You're running out of time."

My attention perked up when, in the kitchen, Uncle Sawyer's name came up. I wondered if they had found him over there in Vietnam. Then I heard Uncle Milford say, "I would do anything in my power to bring him home safe and well," which did not sound like he'd had any good news.

Mom said something that I couldn't quite make out as they went out the back door. Uncle Milford's reply carried better. "We decided that getting married anyway was the most hopeful thing we could do."

I went back to my room to watch them cross to the shed, and Uncle Milford's voice floated back to me. He wondered why our yard looked so scalded. That's when I saw Daddy's truck pull in.

It's funny, the kind of things you know about people you've lived with your whole life. Sometimes you can't figure them out at all, and sometimes you know everything in a heartbeat. I saw a moment pass between Mom and Daddy where they both didn't move. Mom knowing she wouldn't tell him Collin was gone. Daddy deciding he wouldn't let Uncle Milford see they had been mad at each other. Then they all went into the shed like nothing had happened at all.

I wasn't like Mom. I couldn't decide not to tell, and then act like nothing happened. The thought of sitting at the supper table with Daddy and holding in the secret of Collin and my money made me feel weak and trembly all over.

While they were in the shed looking at the buffet, I yanked some clothes out of my dresser and found my hairbrush. I stuffed everything into my book bag. I pulled my sneakers out from under my bed by the shoestrings and beat it downstairs.

As the back door whacked shut behind Mom and Daddy and Uncle Milford coming in, I went out the front. I couldn't stand watching Mom and Daddy fight anymore.

When I came back, I'd have hatched some story about losing my money. Because while I had to say something about what happened to it, I had given up any notion of being truthful. I didn't want Daddy to look at me like he'd looked at Collin and even at Mom lately. Like he wished he didn't know who they were.

I was going out to Grandma's, where all a body had to worry about was showing up on time for supper. As I jumped off the porch, I stepped down on something soft, something that popped under my bare foot. There wasn't a noise to hear, but it felt like a balloon that's down to a last puffy bit that bursts as you step on it.

"Oh, no," I said.

A small toad, about as big around as a quarter, lay in the grass staring calmly up at me. One of its legs had separated from his body, connected now by only a flat white thread. It didn't try to move, didn't do anything terrible like gasping or writhing in the grass.

Sweat trickled down my sides.

I knew I ought to step on it again, to finish it off. It couldn't wonder what was going to happen next. At least I hoped it couldn't. I tried to get behind it. Its eyeballs swiveled so it could keep watching me.

My skin felt scrunched up all over, my whole body tight and ready to face something horrible. I raised my foot, trying to get up the nerve to step down.

I saw the poor thing flinch.

I pulled my foot back. It probably remembered this was the exact thing that had happened only moments before and now look what kind of condition it was in.

I heard Daddy's voice from inside, saying something about going upstairs for a minute. I panicked and ran for Uncle Milford's pickup, my sneakers swinging, and climbed into the back. Ducking under the canvas tarp, I almost changed my mind. It smelled like soured milk. My stomach rolled over—it was partly the smell, but it was more about the toad.

The toad. I couldn't get my mind off of it. I had made a report on toads once, and I knew it would be there till its skin dried out. Slow suffocation.

What with these thoughts and that cheesy odor, and the hot metal of the truck scorching my legs, I cried a couple of big sobs. I felt better and worse both, letting the feelings in and crying them out. I might have cried more, but I heard the squeak of the back door, and Mom calling my name. "Gra-ace!"

"Grace!" Uncle Milford bellowed. I didn't budge.

"I can stay and help you look for her," Uncle Milford said from someplace much closer, so I knew Mom was walking him out to the truck.

"She'll turn up," Mom said, sounding like it didn't matter much one way or the other.

The truck door opened. "Tell Collin we can use his help building my house," Uncle Milford said as he got in.

The truck started. For one moment I wanted to sit up and make light of hiding there. The look on my mother's face would more than make up for any punishment she could dream up. But in my mind, I heard her cool voice saying, *She'll turn up,* and I got mad.

She'd soon change her tune.

14 Reaching the Border

An hour later, I had begun to regret running off. I could hardly breathe under that tarp, even with all the wind swirling around me. Every bump in the road rattled my teeth.

More, I had begun to think.

I didn't want to face Daddy. That drove me down the stairs and out the door. But once the truck was on its way, I could only think how mad Daddy was going to be that Collin had run off to Canada.

He'd be more upset to hear that Mom had helped.

When he got around to me, who, so far as he knew, had only run off to Grandma's—he didn't have to know about my money to be mad—I would be the only one he could actually punish.

At first, it had been my idea to stay out of sight till suppertime, then turn up at the table with everyone else. There was enough going on at the farm that it was just possible no one would notice I hadn't been there that morning. I thought I'd call home around that time.

Now I didn't want to be found out at all. I had to get home before Daddy knew I was gone. That was my only hope.

I knew we were getting near. Time can fool a person, but the air smells different at Grandma's. Green. I hit it right on the button. Uncle Milford slowed, turned, and rattled along a dirt road for about a mile before he stopped.

Peering out, I could see that we were parked under Pop's oak tree in the front of the house. The lawn chairs were empty of my uncles, and would be till the day's work was done. At least a dozen of Grandma's boys still lived around the farm in houses like the one they were building for Uncle Milford. It was only my daddy and Theo's who had chosen to live in town and run a business.

Uncle Milford flipped back the tarp, catching us both by surprise. He yelped and leaped back like he'd uncovered a nest of snakes.

"Hey, Uncle Milford!" I sat up real fast.

"Get outta there," Uncle Milford said.

"Quite a ride," I said. I made a big deal of brushing bits of hay and dirt off myself with shaking hands, giving Uncle Milford and me both a chance to get over the pure shock of finding me there. My face got hot. I didn't need a mirror to know I'd gone an ugly fiery red.

Meanwhile, I noticed there were pickup trucks and station wagons parked all up and down Grandma's driveway, more than usual. That might mean someone could drive me back home before Daddy knew where I'd been. Maybe Mom didn't have to know either, if I got lucky.

I grabbed my shoes and book bag. "See you later," I said, swinging my legs over the side of the truck.

"Not so fast," Uncle Milford said. "You better come inside with me."

Drat.

I followed him across the gravel, hot and knobby under my feet. The grass felt cool and smooth, the porch steps dry with flaking paint. My heartbeat was kind of choking me the whole time. Uncle Milford didn't usually get angry with us kids. For one thing, he was nobody's daddy.

I had never before come to Grandma's on the run either. I had gotten on Grandma's wrong side pretty often, but never in a way that made me feel like I might lose her good opinion of me.

A baby lay fast asleep on a cot inside the front porch, pillows bunched all around it. I was careful not to let the screen door slam. Besides which, I needed the moment to catch my breath. I wanted it to look like I meant to be found out.

In the dining room, my aunts were slipcovering a chair for Uncle Milford's new home. "Hey, Grace," Aunt Birdie said, looking up from her sewing. She pointed at her baby girl, who was toddling across the room. "Stellie's walking."

"Omigosh," I said, trying to make the kind of fuss Aunt Birdie wanted. For a moment, I thought the warm flush on my face might not be noticed. Uncle Milford came back to hurry me along with a hand at my back.

I still wanted to look like it was my own idea to rush on to the kitchen, but he stayed right with me. Bushel baskets full of green peppers and purple grapes cluttered the floor. Two babies sat beneath the table, puckering up as they tasted the grapes. One of my aunts raised her eyebrows at the sight of me.

Grandma stood at the sink, rinsing jars. "Got me a stowaway on the truck," Uncle Milford said in her direction.

She looked over her shoulder. "A desperado? Well, she's come to the right place."

"Her mother doesn't know where she is," Uncle Milford said.

Grandma pointed to the phone on the wall. "Call your momma."

Fast tears burned my eyes. "Do I have to?"

Grandma said, "Right now."

One of my aunts looked up from slicing turkey and said, "Grace, come on over here and tell us the straight story." Right away I didn't want to get close to her, and I didn't even know why.

Aunt Lutie said, "Don't listen to her, sweetie. I told her Collin would never burn his draft card. I don't know how these stories get started."

"They get started when *some*body burns their draft card and the *other* people who were standing around will, later on, talk about it," Aunt Chloris said. "What I want to know is whether Collin burned *his*."

I glanced at Uncle Milford, who didn't look like he'd heard their questions. He didn't look interested in anything but sweet tea, which Aunt Chloris was pouring into glasses, ice clinking.

"Some boys are made for trouble," Aunt Lutie began.

Aunt Chloris said, "*All* boys are made for trouble, and most of them do find it."

"Here now," Uncle Milford said, offended.

"To wet your whistle." Aunt Chloris gave Uncle Milford a glass of tea.

"Not our Collin," Aunt Lutie said, starting to annoy me. "He wouldn't know the way."

Uncle Milford said, "Collin doesn't have the knack for trouble."

Well, this just frosted me up one side and down the other. Once, when I broke a lilac off of someone's bush, we got calls from three different old snoops telling Mom I'd end up in a home for juvenile delinquents for sure.

But not Collin, oh no.

"If Collin held up a bank," I said, and everyone's eyes fell on me, "somebody would make out he only took that money to be cleaned and pressed."

Aunt Chloris gave me sharp look, and Grandma said, "Are you calling?"

I dropped my stuff on the floor under the phone. I dialed hard, fast. I gave my book bag a little kick when I heard the first ring.

Grandma had noticed the babies. "Will someone carry those little'ns back to the front rooms before they choke on a grape?" She called any child under three years of age a little'n. She claimed she couldn't keep their names straight until they were old enough to sass back to her.

Mom answered the phone and I said, "It's me."

"Where are you?" she screamed in my ear. "I have called everyone in this entire neighborhood."

"I'm at Grandma's."

I heard Mom's breath catch. I knew suddenly, this was exactly where she didn't want me to be, right in the midst of Daddy's family. "Grace, I don't want you to talk about Collin," Mom said. "Not one word."

The largeness of what my brother was doing, of what my mother had done, struck me like a chill. Collin could go to jail. I didn't *want* to talk about him.

More than ever, I wished I had not heard Mom in Collin's room. I wished I had been somewhere else so that I would never have known she was packing his clothes. I would never have put my money in his pocket.

"This ought to be your secret," I said in a low voice. "It ought to be Collin's. I don't want it to be mine."

"You aren't the only one caught in the middle," she said. "We all are."

"Just one big happy family."

"Grace. I can send your daddy right out there to bring you back."

I ducked my head. "I couldn't stand to be there when Daddy got home," I said in a lower voice. Tears dropped to the floor. "When he got mad."

"Then stay where you are," Mom said. "Can I count on you?"

I didn't know how to answer. After a moment, I hung up.

Aunt Chloris waited to put me to the test. Could Mom count on me to keep quiet? My aunt handed me a cold glass, wet sliding down the sides. I drank half the sweet tea down in three swallows.

Dolly and Theo came into the kitchen then, fast and noisy. They looked sun-browned and wild. Dolly's glasses had slipped down on her nose and Theo's T-shirt was a size too small.

"Party girl!" Theo shouted, skidding to a stop in front of me.

"Party pooper," I said. My heart settled into its rightful place again. "I had to call my party off because of you. None of the girls would come the minute they found out you weren't going to show."

"Hoo-whee," Aunt Lutie said, making everyone laugh. Theo started for the door, but he was sporting a little smile.

"Hold on there," Grandma said before we could make a clean

getaway. "I didn't gather eggs this morning. It's about time somebody got out there and took care of it."

"Yes, ma'am," Dolly and I said at the same time.

"Take baskets," she called as we skittered out the back door.
"And don't upset my chickens either."

15 JUST US CHICKENS

Grandma's beagle, Lucy, took up with us as we headed for the chicken house. "Did you come out with your mom?" Dolly asked.

"Uncle Milford brought me."

"So?" Theo asked. "Did Collin really do it?" He mimicked scratching a match on his heel.

"You all knew Collin was going to that sit-in, right?" Dolly said. "Why didn't Uncle Wick tell Collin he couldn't burn his draft card?"

I lost my temper. "Daddy told him not to *go* to the sit-in," I said. "He told Collin not to go, and he probably thought that covered everything."

Dolly put on her look of bitten-to-the-quick. She said, "I asked a simple question. All I wanted was a simple answer."

"You got it," Theo said.

I said, "Are you satisfied now?"

"Jeez," Dolly said. "You don't have to get mad."

Theo and I glanced at each other. We didn't have to get mad, but with Dolly we did have to put up fences. The girl did not know when to leave off.

"Well?" Theo asked me. "Did he burn it?"

We were back to the one simple question. I didn't expect this from them, but I should have, I saw that now. I should have thought about what to say. I said, "If somebody told you, it must be true."

"Aw, don't get like that," Theo said.

Dolly added, "People talk, that's all." She offered this up with a "just us chickens" shrug.

"If you're just people," I said, "I guess you can buy a newspaper, like anybody else. Read all about it."

Dolly stopped at the gate to tie her shoe. "I can guess how you must feel."

My mind flipped back to graduation day when Theo's brother didn't show up. I remembered it was Dolly who, when someone mentioned Canada, believed the worst immediately.

"We don't know where Thatcher is," I had said to her then, because at the time we didn't yet know. "We don't know Thatcher ran off at all. There could be some other reason for him to miss graduation."

"Name one," she said.

"Kidnapped by the cheerleaders?" I'd said, hoping to lighten things up. But her big brother Willie had gone to Vietnam, and she was real touchy about the whole subject.

"I'm never going to forgive Thatcher if it's true," she said that day, getting into the car to go home. "I'll call him a coward to his face." Theo heard every word. His face had gone white, except for bright spots on his cheekbones.

Remembering this, I said to Theo, "Good to know you two patched things up. I thought you wouldn't be talking to her."

"You can't pick on somebody if you aren't talking to them," Theo said, "and she does like to pick on me."

Dolly picked up her egg basket, pushed her glasses up on her nose, and headed for the chicken house. Theo crowed like a rooster and ran off across the barnyard, his bare heels flashing grass stains as he passed her.

She looked over her shoulder and told me, "Theo says Collin is trying to get up his nerve to go to Canada."

My stomach went tight, and my voice sounded high, like Mom's. "Don't ask *me* to wonder what Collin's up to," I said.

"I figured," Dolly said, and slowed up to walk next to me. "Don't remind Theo what I said, okay? Don't do that again."

"Then don't bother me about Collin," I said. "Since when do big brothers confide in their little sisters?"

Ahead of us, Theo shooed Grandma's beagle away from a tipped-over garbage can and set it upright. "Git," he said as she darted back and snatched something up off the ground.

Dolly said, "Got a question for you" in a way I knew only too well.

"Not now, okay?" I said. Dolly's questions could haunt a person for the rest of their natural life. "I just got here."

"This one's easy," Dolly said. "If we all three went out in a boat and the boat turned over, who would you save first, me or Theo?"

"Me," I said. "Me first."

I ran ahead to catch up to Theo, who was already collecting eggs.

The chicken house smelled so bad, it took my breath away. The floor was crusty and sticky with chicken crap. Theo looked like he hardly noticed, and I tried to look the same way. I wished I had put my sneakers on, though.

I made myself move slowly, being careful not to jig any of

those hens hard enough to get pecked. No talking, at least there was that. The chickens liked a certain tone of voice or they got nasty.

They wanted a certain mood, a kind of quiet happiness over finding chickens and eggs at all, and I, for one, was not in that mood. I had come out here to find that easy place inside myself, where what Collin did had nothing to do with me. It struck me that that place might well be gone.

"We got enough," I said. I opened the door to find Grandma's dog waiting right outside, whining, sad beagle eyes turned to us. Strings of saliva swung from her mouth.

"Oh." It was all I could think of to say.

But Theo yelled, "Mad dog!" He slammed the door shut. Behind us there were several protests and a general ruffling of feathers. Dolly set her egg basket down, and pushed past Theo and me to open the door again.

"Oh, poor thing, poor sweet thing," she said, hunkering down in front of the dog. She patted everywhere, looking for a sore spot. Lucy whined as Dolly checked her mouth. "She's got a pig's knuckle wedged in her jaws."

Theo set down his eggs with a take-charge air. He got a grip on the back of Lucy's neck and yanked the thing out. It made a little *thk* sound as it came loose. Lucy never made a sound at all.

Theo plunked the pig's knuckle into Dolly's hand. Then he snatched up his egg basket and strode back to the house. The beagle trotted right behind him, tail wagging.

Dolly and I followed more slowly, stopping off where a few of our aunts were caning chairs in a shady spot. We told them Lucy's story, skipping entirely the small part where he screamed "mad dog" and shut the door in the poor dog's scared face.

Theo came back outside in time to hear this, but when he got us alone, he said, "You should've told them Lucy got in the garbage and left it at that. You didn't have to make a saga out of it." And he stalked off.

"If we had been the ones to yell 'mad dog,' he'd have told the story backward and forward, believe you me," Dolly complained.

But I didn't really mind that we were on the outs with Theo. The world had lined up in some right order again that I could settle into. And I was secretly grateful that Collin had been forgotten for the moment.

"Here, you girls," one of our aunts called. "Make yourselves useful."

16 OUR BROTHERS' SHADOWS

We herded five little'ns out to the edge of Grandma's vegetable garden with spoons and old coffee cans. Stellie, and Dolly's little brother Hammie were among them. The soil there was the color of charcoal—clean dirt, easy digging.

Dolly and I picked ripe tomatoes to eat like peaches, juice dripping down our chins. I enjoyed the simple fact of sunshine and a breeze till Dolly asked, "Can I tell you something? You have to promise not to tell your mom."

I said, "What's the big secret, anyway?"

She said, "I saw Uncle Mac give a hitchhiker money."

I felt the prickle of the hair on my arms. After Pop died, Uncle Mac took over running the farm. He wasn't the oldest, but he seemed comfortable with the job. I didn't talk about him in the tone Dolly used.

"So?"

She said, "He let him ride in the back of the truck with us and then he gave him money, you know? To help him get where he was going."

When I didn't say anything right away, she added, "To Canada."

I asked, "Why'd you tell me, if it's a secret?"

"I thought you'd want to know."

"I don't care about the hitchhiker," I said. "I don't care if Uncle Mac gave him a hundred acres. That's Uncle Mac's business, not mine, and not yours either."

"Don't tell me what's my business," Dolly shouted. "My brother is over there and yours will be soon."

I opened my mouth and shut it again. My brother had other plans.

Beside her, Hammie had dug up an earthworm. He held it up to show Dolly, but she pushed his hand away without looking. "What?" Dolly said to me.

"I thought you must've had a change of heart," I said. "You asked me not to remind Theo of what you said at graduation."

"I don't want to fight with him all the time, that's all," Dolly said irritably. She turned to help Hammie dig a deeper hole. "We can't do anything about Thatcher running off. But Uncle Mac doesn't have to help every boy who wants to follow him. That's what Mom says."

"Maybe Uncle Mac remembers what it's like to stand on the side of the road," I said.

Dolly stopped digging to look at me. "Do you know that for sure?"

"No," I said. "But maybe it's true."

"I don't care," Dolly said. "It's not right for Uncle Mac to help boys run off. Willie is over there fighting, and Uncle Sawyer is probably dead."

"Dolly!" The little'ns were by now giving us round-eyed looks. I didn't think Dolly should have said that in front of

Stellie. Maybe Dolly didn't think so either, because she quieted right down.

She plunked Hammie's spoon into the dirt and looked off across the yard, where our aunts were sitting on the kitchen steps. They were peeling a mountain of potatoes. They were laughing.

"They're shooting real bullets over there, Grace, and they're shooting them at our family. What if Willie ever needs help," Dolly asked me, "and help doesn't come?"

With one stiff finger, she poked her glasses up on her nose. "What if that boy was the one who could help Willie and he isn't going to be there?"

Until then, it had not occurred to me to be ashamed of my brother. Dolly would never let me hear the end of it. If she believed Thatcher should have gone, ought to *want* to go, she would feel the same way about Collin. I didn't know if I could stick up for what Collin did.

Or for what I did, if I ever told. I was hatching a plan to tell Dolly that I had lost my money, and let her tell everybody about it. It would seem more believable that way. The only thing that bothered me about it was, it felt worse than putting my money in Collin's pocket.

"Cut that out, Hammie," I said, seeing him stretch an earthworm.

Dolly dumped his can of dirt. "Here, let's make your can rattle," she said. She took him off to the water pump to pick up some gravel, still fussing at him.

It wasn't that we always got along so perfectly, Dolly and me, but we'd never had differences we couldn't overlook. When she came back, I said, "Let's don't talk about it."

Dolly shrugged. We watched Stellie spoon a little dirt down the back of another little'n's neck and neither of us made a move to stop her.

"Does Willie write?" I asked her. I hated myself, but I asked. "Tell me what he says in his letters, why don't you?"

She hesitated, then said, "He reminds us of what he'd be doing if he was here. What he misses. He tells us how pretty the countryside is over there. The sunsets. Daddy sent him some of those paperback Westerns he likes."

"I didn't know they could get things like that over there."

"The army has its own mail," she said. "Once, Willie wrote that he dreamed about the icing on cakes. We sent him a chocolate cake. He wrote that he ate all the icing off the foil we wrapped it in."

Dolly turned away to help Hammie as he came back with fistfuls of gravel. "Here, Hammie, sit down and line them up like a train."

"I'm sorry Willie is so far away," I said. I had never been so sorry.

Dolly said, "Mom says that she tries to do something good and kind every day, to keep Willie safe."

I got angry all at once. "Your mom is always good and kind. That has nothing to do with it."

"You mean you think Willie will get hurt?"

"No!"

"What, then?"

"Here comes Theo," I said, relieved to see him. He was with Dolly's nine-year-old brother, Cliffie, and Ben Joe.

"Don't tell," Dolly said. I didn't know what I wasn't supposed to tell. I didn't have time to ask.

The little boys looked very proud to be chumming around with Theo, big boy him. As they came up to us, they flashed the peace sign at us, all three of them at once, and said the usual sort of things to go with that. "Peace, man." "Power to the people."

Theo added, "Make love, not war," and gave Cliffie the giggles.

"What is that all about?" I said.

"We're demonstrating," Ben Joe said.

Dolly said, "You let your mommas hear you talking like that and you're likely to get your seats warmed. My momma will warm them, anyway." And to Theo, she added, "You read too many books, that's your trouble."

"Maybe we don't think that's our problem," I said. "I don't think you're half as smart as you believe you are. Asking questions that bother people isn't the same thing as thinking."

Dolly pulled one shoulder up in a shrug. "It's a kind of thinking."

"And what kind would that be?" I said.

"It's wondering, and if ever it's a kind of wondering that makes you worry, it's called thinking."

Theo and I met eyes, and in that way agreed to let her have the last word.

17 TRUCE

Dolly and I were still uneasy with each other as we got into the back of a pickup to eat supper. Dolly asked if I would hold her paper plate while she climbed in. Normally we would simply have handed our plates to each other. We wouldn't have to make plans to do it, and we never had to be polite.

"This is a lot cleaner than Uncle Milford's truck, I can say that much for it," I said, hoping she could forget about the things we'd said. Or at least the things I'd said.

"You know what's going to happen?" Dolly said. "All the girls who liked Collin are going to be asking you about him."

This was a scary thought, but only for a second. "He only has the one girlfriend. Kerrie."

"Not his friends," Dolly said. "Yours. How many of your friends had crushes on him?"

I gave her the look of, You've got to be kidding.

Collin wasn't the kind of big brother who ever made my girlfriends fall in love with him. The super-cute one or the funny one? He wasn't even the really nice one.

Willie was the kind of brother who didn't mind that Dolly took a shirt from his closet when she wanted to dress like a railroad tramp on Halloween. Willie made her friends laugh. Before we could get into that, Theo turned up.

He didn't need anyone to hold his plate as he climbed over the tailgate. "How about we make a truce," he said.

I said, "Where'd you lose your Indians, chief?"

"Grandma said they had to show her their hands before they could eat," he said. "I ducked for the chow line while they were showing up in the kitchen."

"Must be an old Indian trick," Dolly said.

"Hey, now," Theo said, "is this a truce or not?"

"You can eat here," Dolly said. "That'll have to be good enough."

Theo told me, "She's been mad at me for two days because I saved you from drowning."

"I asked him," Dolly said patiently, "if the boat turned over, who would he save first?"

"And I said, 'Grace, because she's nearest,' " Theo said.

"It sounds perfectly reasonable to save the nearest person first, Dolly," I said. "Wouldn't you?"

She said, "What I want to know is, why do you get to be nearest?"

"Because I am, that's all," I said.

"You girls get on a person's nerves," Theo said.

There started to be some movement away from the picnic tables in the yard. When a couple of our aunts came out of the house carrying little'ns and diaper bags, I remembered—Friday night was movie night.

"What's playing at the movies tonight?" I asked. "Either of you know?"

Uncle Milford stopped by us as he headed for his truck. But before he had a chance to say anything, Aunt Chloris asked him, "Where is your bride-to-be this evening?"

"She ought to be there at the cafe," he said. "She has the late shift this month."

I crooked my finger at Uncle Milford. When he leaned toward me, I whispered in his ear, "Are you still mad at me?"

"Nope," he said. "But it's real sweet of you to worry about it."

"Milford," one of my aunts called. "This truck ought to be condemned."

"What'd you tell him?" Dolly wanted to know as Uncle Milford shuffled off to defend his honor.

I crooked a finger at her and whispered in her ear, "If I wanted to tell anybody else, I wouldn't have whispered."

One of our uncles made a leap onto the truck bed right then and Dolly had to let it pass. I called out a few hellos, hoping she'd let the matter drop if we could only get on the road.

18 YOU CAN RUN

Nobody talked once the trucks picked up speed, not with the wind blowing all around. The standing corn blurred into a green curtain as we sped past the fields.

The air had changed again, cooling a bit as the sun started to go down.

I couldn't help wondering if Collin was looking at this same pink and lavender sky painting from the back of somebody's truck. I couldn't picture him writing letters about it. I didn't know whether we would be writing to Collin, wherever he went. I thought maybe Dolly was right, maybe this was thinking. Because what worried me was, what would I say to Collin? What would he want to hear?

I had just made up my mind that Collin had no business making me worry about him when we went through a flashing yellow light, and another truck turned onto the road. It was Daddy's truck, and he pulled into line right behind us.

Mom didn't wave, and Daddy didn't either. Somebody pointed them out, and I nodded, Yes, that's them all right. I wanted to turn up my feet and play dead. I thought Daddy must for sure know about Collin by now. I suddenly realized that Mom had probably checked my drawer and knew my money was gone. She might even have told Daddy, not knowing I had put it in Collin's pocket. Somehow this likely chain of events had escaped me before.

I started to dread getting to the movies.

When we slowed down to turn a corner, Dolly said, "It's a long way for your folks to come to see a movie. Maybe something's up."

I shot her a narrow-eyed look. "Thank you, Nancy Drew."

Another truck slid into the space between our truck and theirs as we went through the next crossroads. I couldn't feel their eyes on me anymore, but I didn't feel one bit better for it.

It wasn't too long before we pulled up in front of the grass lot off the main street. The whole town smelled of buttered popcorn and roasting hot dogs.

A movie screen hung on the backs of buildings there, with the faint outline of windows showing through. A pale preview of coming attractions played over it, but the colors would get better as full darkness fell.

Two rows of pickup trucks took up most of the street, facing the screen. Some people, Grandma included, watched from inside their trucks, windows open so they could hear the sound. That was fine, because Claytonville didn't own a busy street. Passersthrough could slow down and ease their way around all the fuss, or simply pull up and see the movie, like everybody else.

I hopped out of the truck, bent on finding a place to hide. Dolly and Theo stayed right with me. The biggest part of the crowd settled themselves in the grass lot, sitting on blankets.

"Here, don't go rushing off now," Uncle Milford said, slowing us down. "Theo, you've been a real help to me lately."

"Thank you," Theo said, accepting four dollars.

"Show these two ladies an evening out. Movies and a bag of corn," he said. "What's left over is yours."

"Grace is a wealthy woman, Milford," Daddy said from behind me. I hadn't seen him coming. I went sick and dizzy. I had to lean against a truck. Daddy said, "She has a wad of cash that'll make your eyes bug out."

"That so," Uncle Milford said, glancing at me. "Well, you three better go on and find a spot."

I wanted to run, but I didn't. I forced myself to walk away. We settled into a space where two blankets nearly met, and we were invited to share so we wouldn't have to sit right on the grass. Dolly said something to me, but I couldn't make out the words.

My mind was whirling. There was a good chance Daddy knew Collin had gone. Then again, how come he looked so cheerful? I didn't believe he'd be talking about my money like it was the ninth wonder of the world if he suspected I'd put it in Collin's pocket either. So I figured he wouldn't be putting my stuff on the porch, at least not right away.

I hardly heard a word of the movie. When Theo whispered, "Let's go," I didn't even care. We edged back into the darker side of the lot, where a narrow, weedy path ran between two buildings and came out on Main Street.

"I can't pay attention when a movie is all talk, talk, talk," Theo said. "I need to see people do something."

"Not a cowboy or an Indian in the whole thing," Dolly said, teasing.

"Hey, you want to go back and watch that movie?" he said. "Be my guest. Here's your quarter—buy yourself the biggest sack of corn that guy is selling."

"No, you're right," Dolly said, ignoring her quarter. "Willie didn't miss a thing tonight," she muttered as we wiped our ankles to get rid of the ticklish feeling those weeds left on our skin.

"Don't you think about anything but Willie?" I asked her. The words were out of my mouth before I thought better of it. I tried to backtrack. "I mean, you never used to talk about him so much."

"I never used to write to him either," she said smartly.

"I'm sorry about Willie, really I am," I said. "Maybe you shouldn't worry about him so much, that's all."

"I see how it is over there on TV," she said. "It's hard not to worry after that."

"I hate to tell you," Theo said, "but I used to think it was a show. Like, *The War Show.* Maybe even a year ago, I thought that. It was always on when we were having supper, for as long as I can remember. It was boring, yak, yak, yak. I never thought it was real."

"But now you know it's real, right?" Dolly said. Maybe she was saying it to both of us, I didn't know, but she was looking at me. "Now that you know it's all true, you worry, don't you?"

Ever since I got it about the sit-ins, I did think about the war sometimes. But then Daddy turned off the TV and Mom would say, "Do your homework." Pretty soon all that stuff fell to the back of my mind like it was nothing to do with me.

I thought it didn't, till Collin burned his draft card.

I wished I still didn't know any better. Maybe it wasn't all Dolly's fault she wasn't as much fun as she used to be. "Mom won't let us play the TV when we're eating," I said.

"Well, you are both hopeless," Dolly said, but without any bite.

We looked around Main Street. Our prospects looked dismal. There were only three streetlights stretched through the town. Claytonville didn't need more. Only the grocery store and the cafe looked to be likely spots for entertainment.

We were heading over to the cafe to say hi to Uncle Milford's girl when Daddy came out. I stifled a groan. "There you are," he said. "Didn't care for the movie?"

"Nothing exciting happened," Theo answered.

Daddy said, "Hey, you kids let me and Grace talk for a minute?"

19 BUT YOU CAN'T HIDE

They crossed to the other side of the street to wait. Dolly kept looking back over her shoulder like she thought she was going to miss something. I wished I could trade places with her, if she was so interested.

Daddy lowered his voice to say, "You have anything you want to tell me?"

I offered up the quickest prayer I knew: oGod oGod oGod.

"Your mother says you hitched a ride with Milford, unbeknownst to him," he said, giving me a hard look. "What got into you?"

Sweat broke cold on my forehead. "I don't much like being at home lately."

"I know things have been tough," Daddy said, "but it would help if you didn't pull any more stunts like that."

"Are you taking me home?"

"If you want to stay out here, you can," Daddy said. "Leastways, till you wear out your welcome."

I knew I ought to have something to say to that. A thank-you or a promise to help out. Something. But I couldn't bring myself to say it.

"Your mom is staying too," Daddy said. "Don't give her a hard time. She likes your grandma to think she runs a tight ship."

"Not all that tight."

"What's that supposed to mean?"

"Nothing," I said. "I'm on the outs with Mom."

"You getting along okay with the other kids?"

I shrugged.

"Well, you got things to do, I see," he said. "Stay out of trouble, hear?"

"Daddy," I blurted out, wanting to ask, Do you know? But I lost my nerve and asked, "Are you going to forgive Collin?"

He said, "This isn't high school stuff, Grace. It's not about car keys and curfews."

"I know that," I said. I couldn't be sure how *long* I had known that.

Considering I'd been thinking the worst thing in the world would be to face Daddy, whether he knew about my money or not, it was kind of a letdown now that it was over.

Daddy walked back to the truck where I could see my mother was watching the movie. I figured she hadn't told him about Collin either. If it had been me, she would have said not telling was the same thing as telling a lie.

Up till then I thought all I had to worry about was keeping secrets. Knowing where Daddy was sleeping, that was one. Putting money in Collin's pocket, that was another. Not telling about Collin, that was turning out to be harder than I thought it would be.

To keep all those secrets, I had to lie, that's what it came down to. Instead of trying to figure out a better way, the right way, to do things, I found myself looking at Daddy differently, through cold eyes.

I had run off to Grandma's because it scared me to think that when he found out what I had done, Daddy would love me a little less. But while I was standing there, I realized I might love him a little less. I had grown a callus over my heart where a softer feeling for him ought to be.

I didn't even know when it happened. It still scared me to think Daddy might feel the same way about me in only another day or two.

"Did he want to tell you anything about Collin?" Dolly asked as she and Theo crossed the street to stand with me.

"Not one word," I said.

"Well, didn't you want to ask him?"

"He wanted to know if you were asking a lot of nosy questions," I told her. "But I said, 'Dolly? Our Dolly?' "

Theo got a laugh out of this, but I wasn't able to smile.

It had begun to feel worse and worse to keep such a secret from Theo and Dolly. It did feel like a lie. I had said enough that didn't tell them the truth that it made no difference. It put me outside the family somehow. It didn't help one bit to know that Mom must feel pretty much the same way.

"How about breaking loose some of that corn money?" Dolly asked. "I want a lemonade."

"Where's this big wad of bucks Uncle Wick mentioned?" Theo said to me.

"I don't have any of it here." The sad truth. "Besides, Uncle Milford told you to treat us."

Theo dug some change out of his pocket and gave us a quarter apiece. "Big spender," Dolly said, pocketing her quarter before he could grab it back.

"Theo Whitaker, is that you?" Theo's attention shifted to a pretty girl as she strolled toward us. She wore shorts and a top that didn't quite meet in the middle. She had an outie. She also had a scab on her knee.

"Hi, Sara Jean," Theo said in a voice not quite his own. Deeper, somehow. Dolly raised an eyebrow to me. "You live here in town?" he said.

"Down the street. You came for the movie?"

"Yep."

"I saw it last night," she said. "It's pretty good."

"I thought so," Theo said. "But I, uh, my cousins here wanted to go for a walk."

"He's nothing if not a sweetie," Dolly said in a voice like syrup.

Sara Jean gazed into Theo's eyes like a deer stranded in the headlights at night. Theo looked back at her in pretty much the same way.

"Really short skirts are still in, you know," I said to Sara Jean, thinking a silent *thank you* to Judy. "If I were you, I wouldn't wear knee socks. Tights—they'll hide all the scars on your knees."

Sara Jean rewarded me with a shocked little gasp.

"Don't mind her," Theo said, shedding a dirty look in my direction. "She's the cranky type."

"I was going to get myself a vanilla Coke," Sara Jean said, turning so she kind of left me standing to the back of her.

"A vanilla Coke would really hit the spot," Theo said.

"Come on, then," Sara Jean said. "We'll beat the rush."

Theo followed her without so much as a backward glance at us. Walked off looking taller somehow.

"Big boy him," Dolly said sourly.

"Looks like we're on our own," I said. "Got any ideas?"

"Isn't that Uncle Mac's truck in the barbershop parking lot?" Dolly said.

We crossed the street. I gave Dolly a boost to get in, and then she pulled me up. We sat quiet for a few moments before she said, "So how are things at your house?"

"Look, Uncle Mac's left his keys in the ignition." I gave them a turn. "We can listen to the radio."

Dolly sat up straighter. "There they go."

We watched Theo and Sara Jean stroll out of sight, and then we stared at the empty street for a long, silent minute.

"You and I used to tell each other everything," Dolly said. "We said we always would. Have you forgotten?"

On an impulse, I gave the keys an extra turn and the motor came to life.

20 A LITTLE ROAD TRIP

My knuckles went white as I gripped the steering wheel. I thought for a moment, then did the thing with the foot pedals and shifted into gear. The gears scraped only a little. Of course, we'd never done it without Uncle Milford. Until now.

"Wait," Dolly bellowed. "Just wait," she said only a little more quietly when I did. She looked grim. She looked at the street where Theo had disappeared with Sara Jean, and then she looked back at me. "Uncle Mac keeps his Sears catalog back here," she said, turning to reach behind the seat. "You can sit on it."

With the spine of the catalog under my butt, I kept the big toe of one foot on the brake pedal and the big toe of the other on the clutch. It would have to be enough. I eased into taking us for a drive.

Dolly reached out and turned off the radio.

I went around to the back of the barbershop and cut across an empty lot to another street. A dark street, since Main Street had the only streetlamps.

"Wait," Dolly yelled. "Lights."

I stopped again and turned on the lights. "Anything else you can think of?" I asked. My heart was beating so hard, it felt like hiccups.

"Why are you going this way?" Dolly shouted.

"We can come around and meet them head-on," I said.

"Okay," Dolly said. She was still loud. "That's a good idea."

I tried to look casual about driving Uncle Mac's truck, but I was flat out panic-stricken. Sweat rivered down my sides.

Whatever made me do such a fool thing, I kept asking myself. What if I hit something? What if I plumb ran out of gas and couldn't get the truck back to the barbershop? I glanced down at the gas gauge to see how much gas the tank held.

"Careful!" Dolly yelled. My hair practically stood on end.

"What?" I yelled right back at her.

"You swerved there for a second. You might run off the road."

"The only thing that's going to run me off this road is you. Could you please stop screaming at me?"

"This is a crazy thing to do," Dolly said in a nearly normal voice.

"Yes, it is. Let me drive, okay? I need to pay attention here."

She was quiet for about half a block, biting her fingernails. Except that I'd never heard noisier fingernail biting. Like she was popping her knuckles. It made me want to laugh. At least she didn't say anything about the way I had drifted to one side of the road. The wrong side.

She said, "We might as well let them see us, as long as we're going that way anyway."

"I will."

She said, "We'll turn on the map light. Then they'll be able to see us for sure."

"Good idea." My hands stayed glued to the wheel like the truck might yet make a dash for freedom. It wasn't going anywhere without me. And it wasn't going anywhere I didn't want to go.

When the road ran out, I could only go left or right. I headed for Main Street. I spotted Sara Jean some distance ahead, on the fringes of a circle of light from a streetlamp. "Turn on the light," I said.

But Dolly had already gone into action.

As the map light went on, I saw Theo lean over and kiss Sara Jean on the lips. "Turn off the light," I said.

Dolly got there before all the words spilled out of my mouth.

She turned to stare at them as we slid past. I couldn't look anywhere but straight ahead for fear of swerving.

"It isn't a movie kiss. It wouldn't be a kiss at all but for the fact their lips are touching," she reported. Dolly was like Judy in this way—she could be counted on to know these things. She added, "I don't think they noticed the truck going by."

I drove straight back to the barbershop and pulled into the same spot with a crunch of gravel. I shifted into park before I turned the key in the ignition, and let the motor die.

My hands were shaking. Really, I was trembling all over as one muscle after another unlocked itself. I thought about what I had done right. I hadn't run the truck off the road, and I had even parked the darn thing.

I'd only begun to be pleased with myself when Dolly said, "We're facing the wrong way."

"What?"

"You ought to turn it around."

"I'm not moving this truck again," I said. "I'm stopping while I'm well off." I pushed the catalog aside and Dolly dropped it behind the seat.

In the background, we heard the movie. It hadn't gotten any better.

"It's probably a good thing Theo didn't see us," Dolly said.

"Probably."

My heartbeat had slowed to a trot when a figure moved out of the shadows in the barbershop doorway. My breath snagged. Uncle Milford.

He stopped at the window on the passenger side and said in his gentle way, "Good to see all those practice sessions didn't go to waste." And then he was gone, silent as a ghost.

The hair on my arms was standing on end.

"He might tell Uncle Mac," Dolly said.

"He won't." I hoped. "Will he?"

"No, he won't," she agreed. "Next time we do something like this, we ought to check who can see us from the cafe."

I ignored this. The chances of me taking this truck for another drive were slim to none. I hoped the chances of anyone else finding out about this one time were just as unlikely.

"What's it like at your house now?" Dolly asked me again. "Since Collin can't come home?"

I told her the simple truth. "Quieter."

"Do you remember telling me last summer that you wished that Collin would go away and give you a chance to, I don't know, to be the center of things?"

"Well, he did," I said in the voice of, So that's that.

"I thought—"

"What?"

"That if you were a little bit glad, you could tell me," Dolly said. "I'd understand."

Hot tears filled my eyes so fast, I couldn't hide them. I wiped my face with the backs of my hands while Dolly found some paper napkins in the glove compartment.

"I'm sorry," she said, giving them to me. "Sorry, sorry."

"It hasn't worked out all that well," I said thickly. "Nobody, including me, thinks about anything else but if he's coming back."

Which, once I'd said it, was truer than I liked to admit.

"It was the same at our house, after Willie shipped out," she said, like it wasn't going to be news to anybody, not even me. It was, though.

"I'm sorry I made you feel bad for talking about Willie," I said.

Dolly's brother had been gone for months, and somehow I had managed not to notice how hard it must be for her. I never even thought to wonder.

She said, "Worse yet after we heard about Uncle Sawyer. Daddy stays up to watch the late news. He's always watching for a glimpse of Willie."

"Your mom?"

"She doesn't listen to the news," Dolly said with a shake of her head. "But she collects sad stories like recipes."

Another question came to me. "How do your folks feel about what Thatcher did?"

"His name never comes up," she said. "It's like they never heard of him. Like he doesn't . . . exist."

I decided maybe I could live with it if Dolly had to tell me how wrong Collin was about twenty times a day—at least until I had to tell her to quit it. I could stand it if she started hating him, as long as she didn't ignore his existence. At least I thought I could.

21 THE TRUTH ABOUT BOBBY BUFORD

Sometime later, we heard Theo whistling, and then the crunch of his footsteps in the gravel. I shoved the soggy wad of napkins into the crack of the seat.

"I been looking all over for you," he said. He opened the driver's side door, saying, "Move over." He swung into the cab like a monkey and changed the radio station without so much as a by-your-leave.

He told us Sara Jean was the prettiest girl he'd ever met. He told us she was going out for cheerleading, should we want to follow in her gilded footsteps. "You're awful talkative," Dolly said. "Where'd you meet her anyway?"

"Her daddy buys wood from our mill," Theo said. "He builds houses. Bobby Buford was going to work for him before he went off to war. Before he came home missing an arm."

"What do you mean?" I asked. Bobby lived next door to Theo. "Bobby's arm?"

"He got a scratch on his hand over there," Theo said. "He said it looked like nothing. It didn't bleed."

I turned the radio off. "So?"

Theo said, "So Bobby lost his whole arm."

Dolly said, "That means they had to cut it off."

"I know that." I guessed it, anyway. "I don't get it, though. Why?"

"Something about the weather over there," Theo said. "It's real humid. Makes it easy to get infections. Jungle rot, that's what they call it."

Like she didn't want to give me time to catch my breath, Dolly asked from my other side, "How could you not know about Bobby? It was in the paper."

"I don't read the paper," I said irritably, "unless it's for Current Events." I felt stupid enough already.

"You didn't have to *read* the paper," Dolly said. "It was on the front page with a big picture. Big headline: 'Local Boy Hero.' You couldn't miss it."

"Well, I did, okay? I missed it." I turned the radio back on.

"Losing his arm don't account for everything, though," Theo said. "He is strange to a turn."

"Strange how?" Dolly asked. She turned the radio down.

"Well," Theo said, "that first time we visited, he sat on the back porch, staring straight out to the alley. His face didn't change, didn't crack a smile, he didn't say word one."

"You think he didn't want you to see his arm?" I asked. If it was the first time Bobby let one of his friends see him like that, I could understand he might feel that way.

"Naw, he was sitting so we saw it right off," Theo said. "His sleeve was ironed crisp flat and folded up and pinned to his shoulder real neatlike. I will say this, it gave me a nasty shock, even though I knew to expect it."

"You think he had an injury to his brain?" Dolly asked. "I've heard there's a lot of that when a bomb goes off. That could make him strange."

"No, he was more of a sad strange," Theo answered. "He wore the shirt to his uniform, with all his medals—he has a lot of medals—pinned to it. He had a tie, looked real neat. Even though he wasn't going anywhere but to the back porch. Like if the president came to visit, he was ready."

I suddenly remembered this time when the dentist pulled one of my back teeth and the hole it left made me feel so nervous, I filled it in with a jelly bean. "Maybe he didn't feel so much like his arm was gone if he wore that shirt," I said.

"Don't be dumb," Dolly said.

"I don't know that that's so dumb," I said right back. I got angry all at once and I didn't know why, except that it was easier than feeling sorry for Bobby Buford. I had done all the crying I wanted to do for one evening.

"I kept all the time looking at that shirt," Theo said, paying no mind to the bickering. "Not a wrinkle on it. It struck me that Bobby must need help to get dressed. He would need someone to fold his tie. He didn't iron his shirt himself."

"So what?" I asked in a mean tone. "Collin wouldn't know how to iron a shirt if his life depended on it."

Dolly and Theo both glowered at me. "Well, he wouldn't," I said.

"Collin could, though," Dolly said. "If he wanted to. Bobby can't."

"Hey, what are you kids up to in here?" Uncle Mac said through the window, making us all jump.

"We're listening to the radio," Theo said.

"Who moved the truck?" Uncle Mac said.

Dolly and I looked at each other.

"Nobody moved the truck," Theo said, becoming incensed. "What do you think we are, crazy?"

"I could've sworn I left it parked the other way around."

"I don't guess so," Theo said. "This is the way we found it."

"Well, just so's I know," Uncle Mac said, like he still had his doubts. He walked away like a man with a lot on his mind.

"How come you didn't hear anything about Bobby?" Theo asked me once we'd watched Uncle Mac go back to the movie. "Collin's gotten awful friendly with him of late."

I knew what that look spoke to. Thatcher had been friendly with Bobby, and now Collin was. "Collin doesn't tell me his business," I said, which was the last thing Theo wanted to hear. "Daddy calls Bobby Buford a troublemaker. He never said a word about his arm."

Theo raised an eyebrow. "Uncle Wick called him a trouble-maker?"

I shrugged, feeling a little like I had tattled on Daddy. "Anybody Collin hangs out with is likely to get called a trou-blemaker these days. Beats calling Collin one, I guess."

"Seems like losing an arm deserves a mention," Theo said, like he might take the matter up with Daddy himself.

22 BABY POWDER

Mom rode up front in the cab as we headed on back to the farm, but I pretended not to notice her. She did the same. I didn't know how long she planned to stay. With all the relatives and the commotion at Grandma's while the house was being built, I figured we might never run into each other head-on until I had to go home.

As we rode back to the farm in the chilly night air, I began to want a jacket. Huddled against Dolly, who fell asleep almost immediately, I found myself worrying about where Collin was tonight, if he was warm. I didn't want to think about him. Yet I couldn't help picturing him sleeping in the back of somebody's truck.

I wondered if he'd found my money. His money, now. But then I thought he wouldn't find it till he changed clothes. I figured Mom must have given him money too, so he wouldn't be going hungry just yet. I felt a little better after I thought about that.

Dolly and I were sent to one of the bunkhouses when we got back to Grandma's. The farmhouse was small, only four rooms with porches front and back. But Pop had built little bunkhouses that lined up on the lee side of the house, four bunks to each place, and his boys had slept out there when they outgrew the double bed.

They had been given fancy addresses by the boys, which were now shortened to the Ranch, the Cave, the Mud Hole and the Tree House. They all looked the same. They were fitted out with bunk beds and wood-burning stoves. We looked into the one that still had a lamp burning.

Aunt Birdie had taken one bottom bunk, along with Stellie. Aunt Lois was draped over the other bottom bunk with her kids. That left the top bunks for us. We took off our shoes and tip-toed in. "Where's your stuff?" Dolly whispered.

"Still in the house, I guess. My T-shirt is long enough to be a nightie."

Aunt Vera Jean stuck her head in, and after a quick look around, whispered, "You two bunk together. I'm taking one." And then she was gone again.

I poked my head out the door and saw the bobbing circle of light from her flashlight only a few steps away. "If you go through the kitchen, bring my book bag out here, would you?" I said, just loud enough to be heard. "Under the phone."

Dolly and I climbed up to a top bunk, where she sprinkled herself so heavily with baby powder that a white mist hung in the air.

I said, "I can hardly breathe."

"It smells good," she said in a lowered voice.

"A little sprinkle on a baby's butt smells good. This is a bliz-zard."

Aunt Lois said, "Do you want to wake these children?

Because I am not the one who will read to them till they fall asleep again."

So we stopped talking, but we couldn't seem to get comfortable. The bunk was too narrow for the two of us, it seemed to me, although it never had been before. There was all that powder to settle somewhere too. I had an idea we'd wake up looking like we'd slept under a snowfall.

"Be still," Dolly said as our shoulder blades rubbed together. "I can't get to sleep with you jittering around."

She was a fine one to complain. "It's like a cloud hanging over us," I said.

"It makes me feel safe."

For that, I had no reply.

Dolly asked, "Don't you do things that make you feel better when you feel scared or lonely?"

"I don't feel scared or lonely," I said, though I felt a little of both the minute she said it.

"I always feel that way lately," she said.

From the bunk below, Aunt Lois said, "You girls quit that whispering. Tomorrow is going to be a busy day."

Dolly changed gears in an instant, saying, "Aunt Lois, if you were out in a boat with your kids and the boat turned over, which one would you save first?"

After giving it a moment's thought, Aunt Lois answered, "I wouldn't go out in a boat with them, alone or otherwise. I can't swim, and neither can your uncle."

Good answer.

"Say if you *could* swim. And you did go out in the boat. It's just pretend. Let's say that's what happened."

"Go to sleep, Dolly, before you give us all bad dreams."

"I've got a question for you," I whispered. "How're you going to sleep once you start making yourself crazy with these questions?"

"They don't make me crazy," Dolly said. "It helps me to fall asleep, letting my mind work on puzzles."

Aunt Vera Jean came in then and turned out the light. We listened to her get into bed, and then there was only the sound of crickets and breathing. Dolly whispered, "If I don't work on puzzles, I think about Willie."

"Here's one for you," I said. "If something feels too private to talk about, does that mean you're ashamed?"

Dolly was quiet for a minute or more, which seemed to me to be a very long time. When I asked her, I didn't realize how much I wanted an answer. Finally she said, "I don't think so. Some things are just private."

Down below, Aunt Lois said, "I'm gonna put you girls out in the grass with a blanket." Dolly didn't say another word and neither did I. Aunt Lois was not a woman to mess with ordinarily, and we had pushed her to a threat.

I let my thoughts drift, or at least I tried to. It was touch and go because everything I touched on made me think of pickup trucks, from the day Collin burned his draft card till I ran off. Each pickup truck thought that came to me, I couldn't help wondering how many people like Uncle Mac had given Collin a ride today.

Until then, I'd just been mad at Collin. I didn't know I missed him.

23 HOPES AND DREAMS

I woke up full of dread, dreaming of Collin climbing into someone's truck. That, I realized as I sat up, was what his life was like now, wherever he was. It frightened me as much as if I were doing it myself.

Dolly woke up right after I did and started sprinkling on her powder. It wasn't enough that the powder made me sneeze; she had, overnight, dreamed up some fresh question to torture me with. I didn't want to find out what it was, so I headed for the outhouse, walking barefoot through the wet grass.

Aunt Chloris was standing in the open shed that sheltered Grandma's summer stove, tending bacon. The sweet smell improved the air. "Morning," she said, and I returned the greeting.

People had been up and around for some time. I could see a couple of my aunts feeding the chickens and the pigs, and Theo was driving the milk cows out to pasture.

Two of my aunts were leaving the outhouse, so I figured there must be quite a line in the house. Not that I could use the toilet in the house. The bathroom had been put in only a couple of years before, and it remained off-limits to grandkids.

Mom came out of the back door just as I passed it. She said, "I want to talk to you."

My mood soured. The sun was barely up, I'd already had a sneezing fit, and there was still enough early morning cool to encourage bugs to hang around in small biting clouds. I didn't want to talk.

"I'm not mad at you for sneaking out here, Grace," Mom said. "I was at first, but not anymore."

"Are you and Daddy still fighting about Collin?"

"*Argue,* say *argue,*" Mom said. "*Fighting* is whenever people hit each other, shoot each other. Kill each other."

I said, "You know what I mean."

Mom said, "I want you to think about the difference."

"Did you tell Daddy yet?" I asked her. It was like a pressure in me. I needed her to tell and for him to know about my money. I had to find out if he was going to go on loving me the same way.

And yet I still wanted to hear her say he would never have to know.

"How is running off to your grandmother's different than what Collin has done?" Mom asked as we reached the girls' outhouse. "You both got scared at something that's too big, too hard to underst—"

"Daddy doesn't know about Collin yet, does he?" I said.

"He might. Mrs. Miller probably has her binoculars trained on Kerrie's house," Mom said. "Sooner or later, someone will mention that Collin doesn't appear to be there."

She was just trying to get me to crack a smile, so I'd feel like we were on the same side. She had been my mother for thirteen years, and I knew her inside out. I said, "Jokes will not be appreciated."

Mom fixed her flinty look on me and said, "Are you really so eager for me to tell him?" I wouldn't look away; I wouldn't give in. I hated her for knowing about my money. I hated myself because I wanted her to keep my secret.

The outhouse was a two-holer, but it had been a few years since I had shared it with my mom. "You first," I said.

"I don't know why I ever dreamed I could reason with you," she said before she stepped inside.

While I waited, slapping at mosquitoes, I wondered whether Mom and Daddy were going to at least be speaking to each other like normal people when I got home. Sleeping in the same room again. But I wouldn't ask. Mom was mad now, and so was I.

When she came out, I said, "I don't see why you have to sound like I'm the only one who's in big trouble here."

"Lower your voice," she said, and I did.

"I'm not the one who packed up Collin's suitcase and took it to Kerrie's. I'm not hitchhiking to Canada." I stepped inside and shut the outhouse door. Then I stuck my head out and said, "I didn't put anybody's stuff on the porch either, let's not forget that."

I shut the door and locked it. But then these other questions came rushing to mind. Why hadn't she fought Daddy that day? Why didn't she bring Collin's stuff back inside? Collin had to know Mom and Daddy would get mad about what he did. But up till the time Daddy put his stuff outside, he was just a boy who had to be home by one o'clock on Saturday night.

I started to cry. I had cried before, but now I cried just for Collin.

It struck me that getting a draft notice was pretty much, in Willie's mind, in Collin's mind, like getting a note to see the principal. They'd go, of course, their feet dragging, their hearts thumping. They would make brave, funny remarks to anybody they met in the hallways, hoping no one would guess they were afraid. They would go, if no one told them they could do something else. They would go.

The way Willie did.

The toilet tissue was inside a coffee can nailed to the wall. I pulled out streams of tissue to blow my nose. I cried quietly but fiercely for a few minutes until another question bothered me: How big a difference was there between what Mom and I had done?

I'd put my money in Collin's pocket; I had done all I could do to help him, which was exactly what Mom had done. I was glad too. Collin was making his way to Canada, and if I had shut my money back in my drawer, I would have felt much worse.

I hoped Collin would write when he got there, wherever *there* might turn out to be. I wondered if Collin had heard of a place to go. But then I thought of Collin's cap, and I knew what he had in mind.

He'd work on cars, which was all he ever wanted to do anyway. Life would be what he hoped for, at least some of it would be. I wiped my eyes, thinking I would say that to Mom and see what she had to say back.

When I came out of the outhouse, Mom was on her way over to the barn. I might have followed her, but Dolly was waiting for me. "I know you and your mom are fighting," she said.

The smell of baby powder was strong on the air. She had two patchy white spots on her neck where she hadn't rubbed it in. When I didn't come up with an answer, she added, "I guess it's private."

"I guess so." Behind Dolly I saw Daddy's truck in the driveway and realized he had probably not gone home the night before. This was a surprise to me, but it also seemed exactly the kind of thing Daddy did. It was just his way to do the opposite of whatever someone expected.

Dolly said, "You've been crying."

"You know, baby powder won't keep you safe," I said.

She looked away, saying, "I don't like the feeling I have without it."

"What feeling?"

"Like things are different now. Didn't you used to think everything was okay? Like your mom and dad kept you safe? Only they don't really, do they?"

"They do," I said.

"They can't," Dolly said. "There's nothing to keep anybody safe. There never was. I know that. But the smell reminds me of when I didn't know it yet." She went into the outhouse and shut the door.

I knew just how she felt, sad to say.

While I waited for her, I wondered if Collin would have gone to that sit-in, or burned his draft card, if Mom wasn't, well, Mom. Marching to her different drummer.

Because in some ways, Collin acted the good boy not only because it was the best way to get the car keys on Saturday night, but because people liked him for it. He liked to be liked.

I wondered if our mom was more like other moms, if Collin would have done what he was supposed to do, like most of the boys.

Like Willie.

"I'm sorry," I said when Dolly came out.

"For what?"

"For bothering you about the powder. The smell is okay."

"Does it make you feel any better?" she asked me.

"Not really."

"Something will," she said. "You just have to figure out what it is."

24 TAKE IT BACK

At breakfast, the mothers with the smallest children got served first and headed for the screen porch. There, the little'ns stood like baby birds with their mouths wide open as the mommas fed them from their fingers.

Dolly and I helped out near the summer stove so we could pick at bacon and hush puppy crumbs as we worked. I saw Mom and Daddy out by the barn, talking. I figured Mom was telling him everything.

I kept an eye on them, and it wasn't very long before I saw Daddy striding for his truck, his trouble face on. I snatched up a bacon sandwich in a paper napkin and ran with it to meet him there.

"I brought you some breakfast," I said.

"I'm not all that hungry," he said, getting into his truck.

I stood my ground, putting on my most hangdog look, to make him sorry. To make him know I was sorry and to let him know things would be the same between us if he let them.

"All right, give it here," he said. "The day is starting off wrong is all."

"Don't be mad at Mom," I said.

"I have my pride, Grace," he said. "The minute you go to

school and somebody tells you your brother is a coward, you're going to find out you've got your pride too."

"What about Mom?" I asked him. "Doesn't she have pride?"

"She's traded hers in."

"For what?"

He didn't answer.

"Daddy?"

"She says she'll be able to sleep at night."

That sounded like Mom, all right. He started his truck and pulled away. The sandwich he held between his teeth as he made a U-turn didn't look like it would be nearly enough to fix his day.

He didn't wave good-bye. I suspected he would have told me this was bad manners if it had been him standing where I was. As I walked back across the yard, it struck me that Mom was right about him. He was awful stubborn. It didn't leave me much hope of things getting any better at home.

It was midmorning before Grandma set Dolly and me free from being helpers. "Odd to see the two of you and Theo isn't with you," Grandma said as she turned from the stove. "In my mind you all come together like a three-legged stool." She raised an eyebrow and said, "However, you all come together some less useful than that."

"Thanks," I said. "You always say the nicest things."

Grandma laughed and sent us on our way.

By then the sun was beating down hard. We didn't want to stay around the house and get stuck playing with whichever little'ns wouldn't take a nap. "Let's go on out to the barn," Dolly said. "Nobody will look for us there."

The dim of the barn as we first entered was welcome, even if it couldn't truly be said to be cool. Dolly and I climbed up the ladder to the hayloft to make nests. It was hotter up there, but quiet. Private. The hay was clean and sweet.

It was always harder to make a nest than I remembered from the year before. It needed a firm backrest and sides, like a good armchair, as well as downy comfort. We were busy for some time before we were satisfied.

Although we chose to rest in the shade, the open hatch let the sunlight in, washing everything with gold. Bright bits of dust floated in the air or settled on our sweaty skin. We made ourselves comfortable with a few last rustlings, and then we were quiet. For about a minute.

"If the whole human race caught a disease and you knew how to invent the cure, only it wouldn't cure anyone in your family, would you still invent it?" Dolly asked me.

Right away, I wanted to know why it wouldn't cure my family. But I didn't want to get her going. I groaned like I was in pain.

"Come on," she said.

"If you're going to start in on something like that," I said, "I might climb right down out of here."

"Okay, okay," she said. "Just give me your answer so I can think about it."

"I'd invent it. Sure. Why not?" I said, to shut her up. "It would still be the right thing to do."

We heard Uncle Milford, somewhere outside the barn, say he was going out to the house later. That he first wanted to work on an old pickup truck Uncle Sawyer had kept running on love and high test. Since Uncle Sawyer had gone to Vietnam, his jobs had fallen on other shoulders.

Reaching the side of the barn, Uncle Milford set to work. We heard him raise the hood, do a little tinkering, swear over it.

Dolly asked, "Do you think it's right that we're having this war?"

"How am I supposed to know?" I asked. "You've already told me how hopeless I am in that department."

"Uncle Milford doesn't have to go," Dolly said.

"I know."

"Maybe he's glad," Dolly said.

"Maybe." I had decided short uninteresting answers were the best.

"Daddy said Thatcher won't ever be able to come home because he's a deserter."

"Dolly—"

Theo, hidden somewhere below, shouted, "Thatcher's an objector."

I looked over the edge of the loft to see him climbing out of the corncrib. He had come back from the cows and then gone out with Uncle Mac after breakfast. I thought he was over at the new house.

"That's the trouble with eavesdropping," I said in the tone of, You asked for it. "You hear all kinds of things you could rather do without."

"Thatcher's run off," Dolly said from her nest. "That's what deserters do."

Which amazed me. I thought for sure she'd back down. Where was that talk of not wanting to fight with him all the time?

Theo took a flying leap at the ladder and was in the loft in two more bounds. "Just so's you know, you have to *join* the army before you can desert it."

"Same difference," Dolly said.

"Might be, Thatcher objects to shooting people down and blowing them up," Theo said. "Same way he objects to getting shot full of holes or blown into a thousand bitty pieces."

"He was scared to go," Dolly shouted.

I said, "Cut it out, both of you. I mean it." They were beginning to scare me, the both of them.

"If you weren't a girl," Theo said to Dolly, "I'd pound you flat."

Dolly covered her face with one arm, but not because he made a move toward her. It was a sure sign she was about to cry, that raised arm. I didn't blame her. I sent Theo the look of, I hope you're happy now.

"Nobody in our house talks about Willie getting shot full of holes," Dolly said in a squeaky voice, "or getting blown to pieces. There's never anything like that in Willie's letters either."

"Now, did I say a single thing about Willie?" Theo said in a tone that was as much truly sorry as it was disgusted with girls who cry. "That won't happen to him."

"Why not? Why can't it?" Dolly shouted. "It happened to Bobby Buford."

Theo reared back, then turned away to scuff around at the other end of the loft, a scowl on his face. Dolly didn't look like she expected an answer from him. Frowning, she fluffed up her nest a little, making it look more like the beginnings of a cocoon. I almost said so, but I thought better of it.

"She talks like she's the last word on anything to do with this war," Theo said to me. "But she doesn't know the half of it, and no one wants to tell her either. Poor little worrier."

"You can tell me," Dolly said. She poked her glasses. "I can take it."

He turned away, like somebody looking for a rock to throw. Then he came back, saying, "Bet you two don't know why soldiers wear dog tags."

Dolly and I turned blank faces to each other.

"So do you? Do you know?" he said, keeping a steady eye on us.

"Why don't you shut up?" I said. Dolly's hand had crept over to touch mine and we locked pinkies.

"Bobby Buford said they shove it between the front teeth so they'll know whose body it is," Theo said.

Theo's words made a picture in my mind. I knew that same picture would be turned over and over in Dolly's mind for a long time to come.

"Take that back," I said. I jumped up and shoved him. "Or I'm going to tell your dad and mine and Dolly's. One of them, if not all three, is going to make you pay."

Theo didn't shove back. A beam ran across the barn, all the way to the back end of the loft. He took two steps and stepped onto it. My heart stilled, and behind me, Dolly's breath caught loud enough for me to hear.

"Betcha I can walk across," Theo said. Boasted, really.

"So what? Uncle Mac does it all the time," I said. My voice came out thin and breathy.

"Betcha you can't," he said, and then pointed at Dolly. "Her either."

Dolly had gone pale. "Theo, don't start."

"I ain't starting," he said. "I'm finishing. You want to talk about scared, let's see who's scared now."

"I don't want to do it," Dolly said in a smaller voice.

"You're chicken," Theo said loudly.

"I don't want to fall off there," Dolly said. "That's not chicken."

"No? But it's chicken to want to keep from getting shot to pieces?"

The louder he got, the nearer Dolly came to whispering. "No."

I hated the way Dolly had made him feel at graduation, and probably very often since. But I suddenly wanted a fight. I really did. "Let's see you do it, big boy," I dared him.

Theo's eyes narrowed into cat slits. "I'll get across and you won't try it."

The beam was wide enough to stand on with both feet together. It was interrupted in the middle of the barn by a vertical beam, so that it was like walking two shorter beams with a spot to rest. Uncle Mac walked it like it was a curbstone.

If I was careful not to look down, I thought I could get across it once.

"Don't do it," Dolly said to me. "You never want to climb trees and you can't go very high if you do." She was nothing if not helpful.

Theo bent his arms into chicken wings and strutted around the hayloft. "Buh-uck, buck, buck, buck." He made excellent chicken sounds.

"I've never been chicken at any of your games," I told him. The truth was, I felt a little sick, but I tried not to let it show. "You first, big mouth."

He stepped out on the beam. He brought one foot down hard in front of the other for a few steps. When he let out a long whistle, I started breathing again. Dolly had come to stand next to me.

Two more steps and he broke into an Indian dance, complete with war whoops, his hair flying with each hop. Dolly's hand gripped mine as we stood in petrified silence. No doubt he'd been practicing. A lot. Uncle Mac walked that beam as if it was a curbstone, but he didn't dance on it. Theo'd had all summer out here, helping out around the farm, and he'd learned a new trick.

Midway he changed gears and began to lurch across in a drunken shuffle. "How dry I yam," he sang, drawing the vowels out. "How wet I'll be, if I don't find the bathroom key."

He ran the last few steps and lounged against the vertical beam like it was a telephone pole. "Your turn."

25 Your Turn

"You didn't finish yet," Dolly screamed.

"Okay, okay." He swung over to the other side of the beam and crossed quickly, sure-footedly, to the back end of the loft.

I didn't give myself time to think about it. I started out taking small steps. Telling myself the beam was more than wide enough. I looked straight ahead, like when I drove, so that was where I would go. But fear crackled over my scalp and down the back of my neck.

Theo did it, I told myself, probably a thousand times. So could I.

I was not halfway across to the vertical beam before I knew I wouldn't make it. The floor of the barn fell away from my eyes. A strange weakness crept through my shoulders. I stopped trying to take steps and just slid my feet along.

Outside, clouds must have moved over the sun. I couldn't see so clearly in the fading light. Sweat washed down my neck, followed by a wave of dizziness. I swallowed and tried to go faster.

"Grace, you can do it," Theo said. He'd begun to sound worried. I took a little satisfaction from that.

The beam felt soft beneath my feet, and the skin on my belly crawled. I felt the beam sag with my next slithering step, but I caught myself, arms out for balance, before I could be spilled off.

"Grace," Theo called. He sounded far off now. "You can do it, easy. Think of it as a strip of tile on Grandma's kitchen floor."

His voice went on, nearly drowned out by the buzzing in my head. I wiped the sweat away from my eyes and peered into the deepening twilight. It came on fast, this darkness.

Everything went black.

"Grace!"

Theo's shout brought me up to help myself. I caught the beam under one arm as I fell, and I clamped onto it. The jolt nearly pulled my shoulder apart.

Somewhere behind me Dolly shouted, "Hang on, Grace! Get your other arm over."

"I'm coming to get you," Theo said.

Dolly screamed, "No, no, you'll both fall!" She went on screaming as Theo started out anyway, but even I could tell he'd lost his boldness.

"What's going on?" Uncle Milford stood miles below me. "Get back from there, Theo."

"I can pull her up."

"Get back!"

I got a cramp in my arm and wailed like a cat. But I couldn't let go.

"Grace." Uncle Milford's face floated beneath me. "Grace. Sweetheart. Are you listening to me?"

I saw him. He smiled, not the terrified grimace that Theo's face held as he tried to will me across the last few feet, but a real smile. "That's it, sweetheart. I know it looks bad."

I felt too dry in the throat to answer him.

"Don't worry, sweetheart. We'll talk when we get you down."

A sob tore from my chest.

"I'm right under you, Grace. I can catch you." And then, "Grace, let go."

I didn't have it in me to do that. I tried, but when I slipped lower, the beam roughed the inside of my arm and I shrieked, part pain, part fear. I was swinging wildly, slipping, and I couldn't help myself.

My name came at me from all sides. "Grace! Grace." I paid attention only to Uncle Milford's quiet voice. "Don't be afraid. I can catch you. I promise, Grace."

Uncle Milford stood nowhere near as tall as most of the boys, and he was skinny as well. Wiry, Daddy called him. I wouldn't have let go of that beam if Paul Bunyan had been reaching for me. I let go of it for Uncle Milford.

I faced the roof of the barn as I fell. I fell fast, knocking Uncle Milford to the floor.

Theo and Dolly scrambled down from the hayloft to help us pick ourselves up. Dolly's face was wet with tears. Theo kept saying, "I'm sorry. I'm so sorry" over and over.

"Me too," I said, once I'd taken stock of myself and knew I'd lived through it. "Sorry."

Uncle Milford drew a long shaky breath and sat up. His shirtsleeve had torn loose at the shoulder. "Think nothing of it," he said, checking his shirtsleeve with trembling fingers. "We've all done it."

"You have blood on your shirt," Dolly told me.

I was fine, really, but the scrape on my arm looked pretty ugly.

Theo said, "I'll get Mercurochrome," and ran off.

I said, "He shouldn't have gone."

"Probably not," Dolly said, but she shrugged. For want of something to do, she checked Uncle Milford and me up and down for broken bones.

"So what was all the shouting about?" Uncle Milford asked us.

"Dolly said—we wondered if it matters why some of those boys are going to Canada," I said. "You know, whether they object to the war or whether they're afraid. Who's going to know the difference anyway?"

"Why, they will," Uncle Milford said. He picked up his International Harvester cap, slapped the dust off and put it on. "All these boys are making hard choices. It don't matter whether they are the boys who go to war or the boys who don't."

"Willie did the right thing, didn't he?" Dolly asked.

"Now, that's a hard question to answer," Uncle Milford said. "I'm sure it must have been right at the time, but then we'll have to see what we think later on."

"What do you mean?"

"I don't want you to upset yourself, Dolly," Uncle Milford said. "But lately I've been wondering if Sawyer did the right thing. Birdie and Stellie need him, if you see what I mean."

Theo announced himself with thudding feet, and handed the small bottle over to Uncle Milford. "'Fraid I failed to make it a secret mission," he said, panting. "Those women treat that indoor bathroom like it's a private room for the queen bee. They were all over me, wanting to know what did I want in there."

Uncle Milford had finished painting the scrape on my arm when we heard Grandma's voice, calling our names. He tightened the cap on the bottle and plunked it into my hand, saying, "You three certainly are enjoying an adventurous frame of mind this summer." His voice held a definite note of admiration.

In fact, only two of us were feeling all that adventurous. Dolly ducked out of sight in one of the calving stalls right before Grandma got to the barn. Theo and I only had time to look surprised at each other before Grandma was upon us.

"I had to see for myself what was going on out here," she said. "Are you children bent on driving me out of my mind?" And with an air of counting noses, she added, "Where's your third leg?"

"Nowhere in sight," I said. Which was the truth.

Theo said, "We were waiting on her, but she never showed."

"There must be a streak of sanity running in this family after all," Grandma said. "The two of you follow me."

When we didn't step lively enough, she grabbed us by our collars and charged full speed back toward the chicken house. I had a glimpse of Theo's feet scrambling in the wrong direction, but Grandma didn't let him fall behind.

26 IN THE BLINK OF AN EYE

Grandma marched us into the chicken house, saying, "Each one of you by yourselves is a fine child, but the combination of you on the loose is more than a body can take. The only thing I know to do is keep you where I can lay my eyes on you."

Chickens squawked and fluttered wildly about until they could escape behind us. A feisty banty rooster followed us around, nipping at our ankles as Grandma chose two birds with stringy necks, giving one to me and tucking the other under her arm.

"Outside," she ordered. There she found two more victims. "Theo, grab that red. The one with the torn foot." Grandma snatched up another one as it strolled past her with a queenly air and handed it to Theo.

I followed them, trying to keep that chicken from pecking at my neck, and when finally I held it upside down, from pecking at my legs. I wished Grandma had killed it already. She didn't favor killing them in the hen yard, though; she said it put off the egg-layers. She had a good-sized tree stump out near the summer stove that she used for a chopping block. She led us in that direction.

Grandma could wring a chicken's neck before it could blink an eye. Then she chopped their heads off with hard, sharp whacks, giving the chickens to Theo and me to hold by the feet, one in each hand.

"Stand over there in the shade of the house," she told us. "No sense in adding a sunstroke to your warts."

We held the chickens out to the side, away from us, the blood dripping in a thin, bright trail away from the chopping block. Blood soaked the dusty earth where we stopped, then splashed onto our ankles. Ants swarmed to the dark, rich puddles of color, then carried tiny drops away.

I saw my mother look through the speckled glass of the kitchen window, but she didn't come outside. She was no doubt hatching some punishment of her own.

"Dolly came out of this smelling like baby powder," Theo said.

He didn't fool me one bit. "I didn't tell Grandma where Dolly was, but you're the one who lied for her."

Theo said, "I didn't mean to get her thinking about Willie."

"A little late to worry about her tender feelings, isn't it?" I asked him.

"I'm sorry," he said. "I am."

"Don't tell me," I said. "Tell her. While you're at it, tell her that wasn't true about the dog tags. Even if it was."

"It was." He gave me a sidewise look. "Tell me about Collin."

I took my time. Surely there were plenty of things to tell about Collin without having to tell more lies. I thought about his cap, still under my dresser collecting dust.

"He's been drafted," I said, and thought about what might be the upside of that. "Daddy's pretty sure Collin could have a job as a mechanic in the army."

"Why?"

"Because he's good at repairing cars, I guess."

Theo looked at me. "You know where Collin learned so much about fixing cars?"

I had never wondered where Collin learned anything. "He always seemed to know."

"Uncle Sawyer taught him," Theo said. "He's a genius with machinery, and they didn't make *him* a mechanic. How could Uncle Wick be so sure that's where they'd assign Collin?"

"They must need good mechanics," I said.

"Sure. They've got plenty of them too."

The ants had started to crawl on my legs, and I rubbed one foot over the other, trying to brush them off. I said, "Look, never mind Collin, okay?"

"You know what Bobby Buford said? His arm still hurts," Theo told me. "Even though it isn't there anymore."

I shouted, "Don't you tell me one more thing about Bobby." Then I saw the look on Theo's face and quieted down. "I don't like to think about Bobby Buford." It was only the truth, but it made me ashamed to say so.

Theo's voice was low and shook a little as he said, "I wish somebody besides Bobby and me could have seen Thatcher the way he was that day. Then no one would say Thatcher was afraid."

"I never thought Thatcher was a coward," I said.

"Yeah, but you don't count," Theo said.

"Collin didn't think so either," I said.

I wondered if Theo knew no one spoke Thatcher's name in Dolly's house. I figured he did. I hoped it wouldn't matter so much to me when they wouldn't mention Collin.

Theo said, "Thatcher put a hand on Bobby's shoulder, the knob of it."

This made my skin creep. It also fell into boy lore for me. The kind of stories where who touched something icky, and who didn't, meant something. Boys thought highly of the strangest things.

"Bobby said most people acted like it was bad luck to touch him at all," Theo told me. "He said they shook hands with him with their fingertips."

I thought of Dolly's baby powder, and saw that Theo had found a way to feel better. He was showing it to me, making me the gift of it. I had to say thank you, and nothing else. Well, except for maybe one thing.

Theo said, "Thatcher made me proud he was my brother. I'm always going to be proud."

"Collin ran off to Canada," I said.

"I know that."

I looked the question at him.

"Stands to reason," he said. "He burned his draft card. He ain't out here helping, and it ain't because he's been arrested."

"You overheard Mom and Daddy when they were out there by the barn, right?"

"I knew before then," he said. "You don't have to listen behind doors to read what's written on the wall."

He shifted his shoulders to lift those chickens before they touched the dirt. I tried to do the same, but my one arm was too sore to fight gravity, and the other one too tired. My chickens hung at half mast.

"You know, I don't think Collin knew he'd cause so much trouble between Mom and Daddy," I said. "It sure came as a surprise to me."

"Aw, your dad's just mad," Theo said. "People say things."

"I know that," I said. "People say things, and then everything is different after they do."

Theo made a disgusted sound and said, "Ain't that the truth."

"Well, at least Daddy knows," I said. Thinking, At least he knows that much. "I guess I don't have to keep it a secret anymore."

"People are going to say Collin ran because he was scared," Theo said.

I said, "Dolly's going to say so."

"Don't worry about her," Theo said. "She doesn't hate Thatcher. She just won't believe he left because he didn't want to kill anyone."

I said, "I'm not sure there's much difference between not wanting to kill people and being scared to."

"A lot of people think objectors are only scared," Theo said. "People don't think killing is wrong if they mostly agree on who to kill."

"I don't care if our brothers were scared and everyone knows it," I said. "I only worry about how we're all starting to hate each other. Mom and Daddy and Collin. You and Dolly. Me and Dolly, the minute she finds out."

"Dad said he never heard of a high school boy who wanted to drive a tank or fly a helicopter who also hoped to get blown up or shot down," Theo said. "It still bothers me, though, when somebody says Thatcher was scared."

"Did we start this fight?" I asked him. "I thought somebody else started this fight and we went over to help."

"Nobody in the twelfth grade started it," he said.

My shoulders ached with the weight of those chickens. As I had given in to it and let them hang lower and lower, the red splotches made a trail that moved closer to my feet. The ants were too many to fight.

"You look hot," Theo said. He kept his chickens at shoulder height. "And white. You look awful white."

"Shut up." I wiped my face against my arm.

"Can't even be nice to you girls," he muttered.

I laughed, then dropped my chickens, running to throw up behind a bush.

Theo pumped cold water over the chickens to rinse the dirt off and dropped them into the water boiling on the summer stove to loosen the feathers. I caught some of the water still pouring from the pump, splashed my face, and left him to strip the chickens. I headed out to the shade of Pop's front-yard oak.

27 Outcasts

Dolly was already there, sitting in the shade. "We shouldn't stick around here," she said. "Grandma's taking scalps."

"Do tell." It seemed to me if Dolly had such strong opinions about our brothers all going to Vietnam together, she should have been there with Theo and me, hanging chickens. "If one goes, they all go," I said accusingly. "What about that?"

She didn't answer right off.

I laid my shaky bones down. Daddy would have said the grass needed cutting, but it felt like cool, dark silk on my skin.

"I should have stood with you," Dolly said miserably. Tears leaked and dropped into the grass.

I wasn't exactly mad at Dolly, but I wasn't quite ready to let her off the hook either. My arm hurt, and by her rules, everybody's arm should hurt. I wanted her to think about that.

"You know what I was thinking about Mom wanting to be good and kind?" she asked. "How can I be sure it works?"

"What?"

"Maybe if I did something weak or cruel, I could wait and see if nothing happens to Willie," she said. "Only I couldn't do something cruel."

"Are you telling me you hid from Grandma to test whether Willie would get hurt?"

"No. I'm telling you what I thought of *after* I hid from Grandma," Dolly said. "I'm sorry, I feel really bad about it. But once I did it, I got to thinking."

"I cannot stand this," I said.

"It's not really proof, I know," Dolly said. "What if something does happen to Willie? I'll feel like he would have been safe if I didn't hide, if I had been really, really good."

"Don't get started on that," I said and rolled away from her.

"My head hurts so much," Dolly said.

I said, "It's all that thinking you do."

The screen door banged and I turned my head to see my mom. "Are you all right?" she asked me.

I felt bad enough before, but after talking with Dolly, all I wanted was to curl up into Mom's lap, the way I did when I was little. I didn't tell her that, though. I said, "I'm fine," like I didn't feel anything at all.

"She scraped up her arm real bad," Dolly said.

Mom said, "Let me see." I turned my arm to show her, trying to look like it didn't matter much.

She looked at it and, as if to say it didn't matter at all, went right on to say, "Well, Milford's done as much as I could. A Band-Aid isn't going to cover that."

"Maybe an aspirin," I said. I was right on an edge, one my mom and I had negotiated before. It wouldn't take much effort from her to sweeten me up, and I hoped she would make the effort.

She looked at me thoughtfully, the way she sometimes did when a change of mind was on the way.

"A baby aspirin," I suggested. "Dolly has a headache. She could use an aspirin too."

She said, "Your dad and I talked."

This was the real reason she had come out here. After all, she knew I was going to live. I said, "*Argued,* you mean."

"Sometimes that's how disagreements are resolved, Grace."

"That's pretty much how Daddy feels about the war," I said, and I heard a little gasp from Dolly. "That it's a disagreement."

Mom said, "Do you think we could avoid taking sides?"

"It doesn't look like it to me," I said. "But I'm trying."

Mom stood there for a moment, but I ignored her.

I didn't look in her direction as she went back inside either. I thought I would feel good about not taking sides, but I didn't. I felt so alone. Dolly gave me a well-what-is-that-about nudge. Theo came around the house right then.

"I brought you a cold cloth," he said with an air of coming to my rescue. He had, only he didn't know it.

"Thank you."

Before I could reach up for the washcloth, Dolly grabbed it and pressed it against her own forehead. "She has a headache," I said.

Theo snatched the cloth off her head and slapped it on mine. "Let her go get her own cloth then."

"I mean it," I said, although I kept the cloth. It felt so good. "Dolly feels awful."

"Yeah?" he said. "Who cares?"

I laughed. I loved Dolly again, and Theo too. It was in the spirit of the moment that I said, "She's afraid if she isn't good and kind, Willie—" I paused here, trying to think of the right way to put it without using the words *hurt* or *die.*

"What?" Theo asked.

Dolly grabbed my arm—not the sore one, lucky for me. "Don't tell," she said.

I said, "She's trying to be *good* so Willie will be *safe*."

Theo's reaction didn't disappoint. "Have you gone feeble-minded?" he said to her. Loudly.

Dolly's chin jutted out.

Theo said, "It won't make any difference whether you're good or not."

"You don't know for sure," Dolly said.

Theo said, "Look, Willie doesn't deserve to get hurt. So he can't deserve *not* to get hurt either. Don't tell yourself it makes any difference, that's all I'm saying."

I didn't know why I didn't think to say something that smart. However, Dolly greeted the good news with silence. After a moment, Theo added, "Nobody can be good all the time. That's why God's in charge of stuff and we're not."

She said, "I have to think about it."

"Don't think," I said.

Theo said, "There's nothing wrong with wanting Willie to be all right."

"Thatcher too," Dolly said. "I worry about him too."

"Thanks," Theo said, and he seemed to mean it.

"Are you sorry he didn't go to Vietnam?"

"No," Theo said. "I'm not."

Dolly asked, "So Thatcher doesn't call you all?"

"I told you—"

"Dolly!" I didn't know why Dolly's question bothered me so much; it was no different than I had done, asking her about Willie's letters. Worse than that, I found I really wanted to know the answer. Not only did I want to know *if* Thatcher called, I wanted to know he *did*.

"This is between us," Theo said to me. "Butt out."

"I only wanted to help," I said.

"You can't," Theo said. "It'll get better or worse, but you can't help."

I wanted to remind him it was no longer just between them. I had a stake in this too. But I hadn't yet told Dolly about Collin, and I didn't want to at just that moment.

Grandma came around the corner of the house carrying a basket of dirty sheets collected from the bunkhouses. "I don't know why God saw fit to give so much free time to people who don't know what to do with it," she said.

Uncle Mac came out of the house carrying a big cardboard box on one shoulder. As he held the door open for her, Grandma said, "Take these woodpeckers out to help at the house this afternoon."

A frown settled over his face, over his entire posture, as he hefted the box into the back of his truck. He looked like he'd rather hang chickens than take us anywhere.

He pointed to the truck and said, "Park yourselves right up there behind the rear window. No standing, and don't throw nothing off the truck, you hear?" Uncle Mac was a repeat pointer, so that his arm and hand looked like the head and neck of a pecking duck. "Do. You. Hear," he said.

"We hear." This was Theo.

We clambered over the tailgate while Uncle Mac went back inside the house. "I bet he's trying to get out of taking us along," I said.

"Fat chance," Dolly said. "Grandma's mind is made up."

Theo sniffed the air over the cardboard box he was leaning against. He broke it open and passed us sandwiches wrapped in waxed paper. While we spread the paper over our laps, he found a bowl with deviled eggs and offered them too.

"He makes a good hostess," I said.

Theo said, "Can it."

Dolly and I glanced at each other. We'd wait.

We ate most of the way through our sandwiches before Dolly said, "He eats like a snake."

"Hardly bothers to chew," I agreed. Like we'd planned it beforehand, Dolly and I took tiny bites and chewed them down to the faintest taste before we swallowed.

Theo promptly snatched a deviled egg off Dolly's lap. "Piggy too," she said. It was in her voice that she didn't mind him in the least.

I said, "Boys will be boys."

"So I've heard," Theo said in a satisfied tone.

Uncle Mac came back out, letting the door slam behind him. Dolly balled up our waxed paper and shoved it into the box. Uncle Mac got into his truck without saying a word to us. He acted like he hadn't noticed we were there.

Theo got in a last word as the motor started. "Uncle Mac looks like his day has taken a turn for the worse."

We rumbled on down the driveway, which always served well enough to cut conversation down to nothing.

28 LOVE APPLES

Uncle Mac drove country roads like he was skimming over a highway, which made for a bumpy ride in the back. We clenched our teeth and spent most of the ride keeping stuff from rolling or jouncing around. I was grateful the ride was short.

This was the first time I'd seen the house going up. It was set right at the edge of a field of cow corn, not a tree in sight. Several men worked on and around the unpainted house. Most of them were our uncles or cousins, too old to get drafted. They were putting in windows and nailing down dark blue roofing. I spotted Caboose right away, so I knew Daddy hadn't gone back to town yet.

Uncle Mac parked in a line with the other trucks. He left us sitting right there, and seemed to have forgotten the lunch box. He headed over to the house.

Daddy was there, helping with the windows. Maybe he was hanging around to smooth things over with Mom. Dolly's dad was there too.

Uncle Mac went up to them to lend a hand, and I saw something happen.

There were no words, nothing easy to explain, but I saw that

Dolly's dad walked away right after Uncle Mac joined them. My guess was, Dolly's dad knew Uncle Mac gave that hitchhiker money. I got that tightening in my middle, part fear, part anger, that had become way too familiar.

"Let's get these sandwiches out of the sun," Theo said.

Dolly and I each took a side of the box when Theo lifted it over the side to us. We carried it to the front steps. Walking away from Uncle Mac and the others, Uncle Milford spotted us and came over.

"Hoo, boy, been sent out here to give somebody else gray hair, have you?"

"That's about the size of it," Theo said. He was carrying a small keg of nails that had been on the truck too.

Uncle Milford sent him into the house with the nails. "You girls come over to my truck with me," he said. "I have a little job, ought to keep you out of trouble."

He had half a dozen buckets on the truck bed, each of them holding full-size tomato plants, a little wilted. Uncle Milford handed them to us, and Dolly and I set them on the ground. They were heavier than I expected them to be, and when we set the last one down, it landed hard.

Uncle Milford thumbed the air in the direction of a garden patch.

"The soil's already been dug through over there," he said as he climbed down. "I'd like you to plant these tomatoes for my girl. Your aunt, pretty soon."

"Digging's pretty hard work," Dolly said, not at all softened. It was hard to impress us with the thought of another aunt in the making. "It's awful hot out here."

"Give them plenty of water, then," he said.

"Why are these tomatoes so important?" I asked.

"Because we want apple trees out in back of the house," Uncle Milford said. "It's too late to put in trees this year, but I figured these for a promise that that's the first thing we'll do next spring."

I grabbed a shovel and passed it to Dolly. I was willing. I owed Uncle Milford. Besides, this was no time to get whiny. We didn't have to carry nails, and we were, after all, supposed to be helpful. And, although I didn't want to look like it mattered, Daddy was on his way over to us.

Dolly took the shovel but she didn't move, not even when I lifted one of the tomato plants off the ground. She asked, "Why plant tomatoes if what you want is apples?"

"Tomatoes used to be called love apples, that's why," Uncle Milford said. He got a pretty pink flush to his face as he realized Daddy had come up behind him and heard that.

Daddy poked him with an elbow. "Used to be people thought they were poisonous too."

"You've forgotten how it was when the old love bug bit you," Uncle Milford said, "back in the Dark Ages." Uncle Milford started to scuffle with Daddy.

I set the tomato plant down and watched them playing around like boys.

Uncle Milford pushed Daddy back a few steps, and Daddy gave in with a little laugh.

"So, can I count on you girls?" Uncle Milford said, having won his battle.

"Yes," I said. Dolly didn't look happy about it, though.

"Put them to work," Daddy said over his shoulder as he went on back to the house. "Around here we earn our dinner."

Dolly rolled her eyes, but we both reached to pick up the same bucket. Without a word, we decided to carry them that way. Between us. One at a time.

"Tell you what," Uncle Milford said, coming along behind us with two more. "I'll get Theo to do the digging for you."

"Okay," I said.

I noticed Daddy had set to work with Dolly's dad on cutting some boards to size. They were talking, anyway, even if they weren't smiling like some of the others I could see. I wondered if that would change as soon as Dolly's dad found out about Collin.

Telling people was probably something Daddy dreaded. I knew he'd said he couldn't hold his head up in town. I had not really thought about him feeling embarrassed when he was with family.

It was something that, like Dolly said, I did not think about nearly enough. Or had not, anyway, before she made me. It was hard to imagine Daddy having the same nervous feeling in his stomach that I had, yet it seemed likely. As we carried another bucket over to the garden patch, I knew Daddy was waiting for the right moment to tell Dolly's dad, the way I was with Dolly.

Dolly made a few halfhearted jabs with the shovel and found the soil was loose enough to dig with our hands. "This isn't so bad," she said.

"So dig a hole," I said.

She pulled up a couple of scoops of dirt, then leaned on the shovel. "Got a question for you."

"No, I've got a question for you," I said. I was trying to coax the first plant out of the bucket without knocking off the tomatoes. It didn't have enough left to brag about. "Since when is it any of your business if Thatcher calls home? Who are you going to tell?"

"Nobody," Dolly said.

"I'm not so sure about that," I said, "and I bet Theo isn't either."

She asked, "You mean you think Thatcher does call?"

I narrowed my eyes at her. "You liked Thatcher perfectly fine till graduation day, didn't you? Theo's your best friend next to me."

The plant finally pulled free. We stuck it in the shallow hole she had dug and piled some dirt over the roots.

"Theo and me," I said, "we're trying to get used to the idea that people you care about don't always do what you think is right."

"Do you mean Collin?" she asked, which caught me right in my middle.

I stood up and brushed myself off. I managed to sound almost regular when I answered, "I mean Daddy. I don't think he did right to throw Collin out."

"Let's go bring the other buckets over," Dolly said. "Leave the planting for Theo."

We started back to the truck for the last few plants. "That goes for Uncle Mac too," I said. "He's going to give more money to hitchhikers, I bet, and you know what? He's still going to be your uncle."

"Better check with him on that," Dolly said. "He didn't look that enthusiastic to me."

I said, "Yeah, he did seem a little moody." Neither of us made a move to pick up another plant when we got to the truck.

There was not a single thing I could think of that would make Willie safe or Thatcher and Collin more right or wrong than they were. But Mom was right about one thing. It would be better for everybody in our family if we didn't have to take sides.

I said, "I'm just trying to say, I don't think Willie and Thatcher meant for us to fight over this."

"It sounds fine when you put it like that," she said. "I don't want to be on the outs with Theo all the time. I know Thatcher didn't want Willie to go. But it still isn't fair for Willie. It won't ever be fair either."

"You've let this war into your heart. "

"What if I have," she said. "What's wrong with that?"

"What if Willie and Thatcher are still friends after the war is over?" I said. "Will you forgive Thatcher then?"

"I don't know," Dolly said.

"I haven't done much thinking about this," I said, "but one thing I see is, war needs an enemy."

"So?"

"Mom always tells me to pick my friends carefully," I said. "I guess if I were choosing enemies, the same rule would stand."

29 Into the Light of Day

Dolly and I weren't sure whether we were having a fight or not. I surely didn't want one. Dolly, as far as I could tell, was still making up her mind. She knocked a tomato plant out of the bucket.

Theo came over then and said, "You girls are going about this all wrong. You have to dig the holes first. I'll help you put your plants in, but you have to do your own digging."

Dolly and I looked at each other. Theo was supposed to do the digging, and we knew he knew it. He started pinching off the wilted leaves on the plant I had pulled out of the bucket.

"You better get to it," he said.

I didn't want to hear all about how girls couldn't do their own hard work. Besides, the soil was light and crumbly. I dug a little trench. Dolly tried to knock another plant out of the bucket while Theo set in the one he had cleaned up. He did a careful job of it, mounding the soil up over the stem, a frown between his eyebrows the whole time.

The next time I lifted the shovel, the dirt did a strange thing. It moved. It wiggled and writhed. "Look at that," I said as it happened again. The dirt acted sort of snaky, but all in one round mound that rested on my shovel so it looked in some way not so scary.

Theo sat back on his heels.

We heard a sound like a little sneeze. And another. And another. A small animal separated itself from the mound of dirt. Tiny paws came up to scrape over its face the way kittens clean themselves.

"Bunnies," Dolly said, dropping to her knees.

It was the smallest rabbit I'd ever seen. The ears were folded close to its head, like thin pleated paper. It felt around in the dirt blindly, as if it didn't know what to make of the warmth of the sunlight.

Another rabbit shook itself free and cuddled up to the first one. Dolly reached out to pick them up. Their eyes were still closed.

"Don't touch," Theo warned. "Their momma might not want anything to do with them if they smell of humans."

"So we ought to bury them again," I said.

Theo said, "They weren't buried. You stuck your shovel into the burrow and it fell through." He spotted an empty nail barrel, short and wide, and dumped the last few nails out in the grass.

"Slide your shovel out from under," he said. "But leave the rabbits up on top of the dirt."

Theo carefully set the barrel over them. "There," he said. "Now the mother can burrow under to them, but they ain't lying out in the open either." He'd forgotten about making Dolly and me dig our own holes, and started to dig a long trench for the rest of the plants.

While I put in another tomato plant, Dolly began hilling dirt around the edges of the barrel. "Where'd you learn to do this?" she asked.

"Collin," Theo answered. "He saved some rabbits in a grass nest this way last summer. The dogs did some digging around it, but they gave up after a while."

"Collin?" I said. Collin-who-couldn't-be-nice-to-me? "Sometimes I think he must have a twin I don't know anything about."

"Aw, Collin's all right," Theo said. "You're just awful hard on him."

"Me? How am I hard on him?"

"I've heard your list of complaints," Theo said. "Not that you're wrong, necessarily. But Collin has a few good points too."

I couldn't make up my mind whether or not to be insulted. Meanwhile, Dolly said, "Do you think they'll really be okay under there?"

Theo said, "That momma rabbit is going to see her babies are fine once we're gone. I don't think she's going to mind the tomato plants at all."

"Theo?" Dolly said, in a little girl voice. "Theo, I know you said Thatcher won't call, but you didn't say *why* he won't." I shot her a warning look, but she said, "I just need to know."

Theo said, "Because he feels like he did wrong."

"Then why did he go?" Dolly asked, her eyes filling up with tears. I forgave her a little bit when I saw that, and maybe Theo did too. "Didn't he know he'd be sorry?"

"I said he *feels* like he did wrong," Theo said. "But I don't think he's sorry either."

"What do you mean?" I asked.

"I think it's possible to do something you know is wrong and you don't feel sorry. I think you have to think what you did is important somehow."

Dolly asked, "How could it be important to do something wrong?" She was beginning to sound more like her old self. I thought we could do without too big a dose of her old self at just that moment.

"Like the Revolutionary War, for instance," Theo said. "People got mad about tea taxes and stuff and said they'd had enough. But I don't think everybody felt real clear about whether they did the right thing till later."

I hoped Dolly would let that lie. But no. She'd no sooner opened her mouth than I butted in, saying, "I don't think Collin thinks about things like that. He only talks about girls and baseball."

After I said it, I knew I was wrong. That *used* to be what Collin talked about. All the fighting started around our house when Collin started talking about what he thought was right. I remembered the papers in his drawer. It came to me suddenly, and I wished it hadn't, that maybe Collin did worry about dying, maybe he thought about a lot of things he never said out loud.

Dolly said, "Can I tell you all a secret? That you never can repeat?"

"Sure," Theo said.

"Willie didn't want to go to Vietnam."

Theo gave her a hard look. "No?"

"I heard him crying in his room the night before he left," she said. "He wanted to stay home really bad."

"Oh, Dolly," I said.

"I'm sorry Willie's there," Theo said.

"Me too," Dolly said. "I think he was really scared."

"Everybody's scared, Dolly," Theo said. "That doesn't mean Willie isn't brave."

"You think so?"

"Theo's right," I said. "I think it's scary to do what Thatcher did, but it's even scarier for Willie."

Dolly said, "Momma wrote Willie about Thatcher."

"What did Willie write back?" Theo asked.

"He said, 'Good.' "

I waited, expecting something more. When it didn't come, I said, "That's it? Just the one word?"

Dolly nodded. "You know what seems strange to me now?" she said. "No one said all that much about it when Uncle Sawyer left. We didn't see him off or anything. He was gone for a month or more before I noticed."

"Because he wasn't drafted—he signed up," Theo said. "He said he wanted to go."

"I can understand 'have to,' " I said, "but I don't know why anyone would *want* to go." Like the first words pulled the rest of them on a string, I said, "Collin went to Canada."

Dolly shrugged. Maybe, like Theo, she had in some way known it all along.

30 A Reminder

In the middle of the afternoon, we hitched a ride with Uncle Mac to get back to Grandma's. We were greeted like the long lost, and we very shortly found out why. The little'ns had had a run-in with Popsicles. Their tiny arms and legs were striped with dirt and colored sugar syrup.

We could tell there'd been a decision made to work us to death.

"Hang your shoes on the picket fence," Aunt Birdie said, putting two wrigglers in our arms. "And make sure you keep counting noses."

There were two washtubs set up out near the summer stove. One tub held wash water and one held rinse water. Getting them into a tub was no trouble. They were so sticky they could be glued together in a clump. The way Aunt Birdie had things planned out, one person would be holding a towel to take each little'n in hand as they were finished dunking.

The idea was good enough, it just didn't take into account the wailing, thrashing, playful little'ns. Once they hit the soapy water, the sugar made them more slippery than greased pigs. They slithered from one side of the tub to the other, never in hand long enough to be truly washed.

Theo sat by a stack of towels, waiting to dry them off as we handed them over. When he saw that we would not be handing them over anytime soon, he said, "You girls are naturals."

"Natural what?" Dolly asked.

"Naturally helpless," he said, and got up to help.

He pulled a book out of his back pocket and left it by the towels. I recognized the black cover. It was the same book I'd taken from Collin's room. I wanted to ask him about it, but I'd have to wait for the right time.

Theo turned out to be surprisingly good with little'ns. He kept those he was handling in a constant state of giggles. He held Hammie up by the ankles, so that shampoo did not run into his eyes. Dolly and I let our eyes meet over this only once, in agreement that we could never have gotten away with it.

Every now and then a wet little'n got loose and ran around the yard, picking up so much grass and dirt we hated to put that one back in with the cleaner ones. Dolly hit on the very thing that made them all want into the tub at once. She shampooed Stellie's longish hair and shaped it into a tall spike.

" 'Poo! 'Poo," Hammie cried until he had short spikes all over his head.

They all wanted to be shampooed so their hair could be twisted every which way, but not one of them would hold still for a rinse.

I noticed Dolly was being nicer to Theo too, as if she'd begun to forgive him for having Thatcher for a brother. I thought maybe those baby rabbits had helped change her opinion of him in some way.

An hour later, several clean and towel-dried naked little'ns were tearing around the yard, their thin hair floating on the breeze. We were soaked through, but we looked like we needed a wash ourselves. The ground around the washtubs had grown nearly as muddy as the pigpen.

Dolly sat on the edge of the washtub to clean up, but I wanted fresh water.

"Why are you carrying that book around?" I asked Theo as we went over to the pump to wash the mud off our legs.

"It's Thatcher's," he said as if the subject were closed.

I let it go at that.

But then he said, "It's hard to explain. It's about this guy who goes off to war and comes back all broken up. He's got no arms and legs. It makes you sorry he didn't get to die, because he's surely never going to live a life. I keep hoping if I read it over and over, I won't feel quite so bad for him."

"It's only a book," I said, because I thought that would help.

"Not anymore," he said. I could see right away that I had slipped in his eyes. "Just because it's a book doesn't mean it isn't real."

"I just don't want it to bother you so much," I said, hoping that might make a difference. "Collin was reading it too, and it must have bothered him a lot." We pumped some more water and stuck our legs under the flow.

"Well, don't you read it, that's my advice," he said, looking away as if he might never look back at me again. "It gives me nightmares."

I was still sort of breathless with feeling cut off from him. We used to forgive each other our differences, but forgiveness didn't come easy to any of us lately. I asked, "So why are you carrying it around?"

"To remind me that maybe Thatcher did the right thing."

■ ■ ■

Over supper, all the talk around us was teasing and foolery. Theo was distant with me, but not so anybody else would notice. Except Dolly, who thought he was in a snit.

He carried a trash can around to clean up the paper plates. He didn't even wait to be asked. After a glance at me, Dolly settled into torturing him. "So how long have you had your cap set for Sara Jean the Glorious?" she asked him.

"Aw, now, there's no reason to go picking on Sara Jean," Theo said, and he slapped his leg. The bugs had started biting.

Daddy came up behind us and said, "Think you about wore out your welcome here?"

My shoulders pulled up tight. "Hope not."

He went around the table and sat down across from us. He said, "My advice would be to leave early, let them get to missing you a little bit. Then come back for a big finale. Burn down the barn or something."

"Funny," I said. But I didn't laugh.

Daddy didn't say anything for a minute. Dolly filled in the gap. She said, "Uncle Wick, got a question for you."

"No," I said, putting a hand on Dolly's arm. "I've got a question for him."

Daddy's look gave me the go-ahead.

"If Collin were here now," I asked, "would you do different?"

"Probably not," he said, color coming to his face. "It's not as simple for me as it is for you." I might have left it at that. I'd left things alone before. But I couldn't do that this time.

"You'd still lock the door on Collin?" I said. "Even after the way things turned out?"

"I was wrong, I know that now."

"Then why?"

"Look, Grace, you know how long your brother and I have been at odds," Daddy said in a low voice. "At first, I didn't know how to treat him like a man, your mom was right about that. Later, I didn't know how to stop fighting with him."

"Don't say *fight*. Say *argue*."

"You sound like your mother."

"Guess I do."

"I know it's no good saying I'm sorry," Daddy said.

"Why not?" Dolly asked. She was folding her paper napkin into ever smaller squares. "My dad says there's nothing saying sorry won't help, even if it only helps a little bit."

I said, "Thank you, Uncle Borden," and I meant it.

"I'm not happy about the way things finished up," Daddy said.

"Maybe we aren't finished," I said. "Maybe there'll come a time when you can say something to Collin, fix things."

"It's late to have my say," Daddy said. "And maybe it's just as well."

My throat felt tight and sad, and my voice came out deep. "I meant you might say something different."

"Like what?"

"Like you're sorry things turned out this way."

Daddy gave me a long look, but it was not the look of a window opening and letting in new ideas, sorry to say. "We'll see," he said.

I hadn't thought to come clean, but it suddenly felt like the right time. "I don't have my bankroll anymore."

He didn't ask what happened to it, he just sighed.

31 | HEART TO HEART

"Let's go sit in the bunkhouse," Dolly said, waving away a mosquito, "before we get bitten up."

On the way, I told her of Judy's newfound glamour. I didn't have to make it sound worse than it was; it was bad enough already. When Dolly laughed, I threatened to tease her hair into an egg shape while she was sleeping. She shrieked as she opened the door to go inside.

"I didn't mean to scare you," Mom said from where she was lying on a bunk, reading one of the little kid's books that Aunt Lois had left there.

"Oh, you didn't," Dolly said. "It was a hairdo story that gave me these goose bumps."

"You must mean Judy's hairdo," Mom said.

We went on inside and shut the door against the bugs. There was very little light from the one window, but it was enough that we didn't have to bother with the lamp. "Why aren't you outside with everybody else?" Dolly asked Mom.

"I felt talked out after supper. But I hoped Grace would end up here," she said, sitting up.

"Daddy's still out there," I told her as Dolly and I crawled into a bunk. I pulled the pillow up close and rested my chin in it.

"You don't have to worry about telling your daddy," Mom said. "I put money in your drawer. I don't want you to spend it, though. Not one penny."

"Thanks," I said, and felt an odd relief. "But I told Daddy it's gone."

"Well, good for you," Mom said, smiling. Good daughter, me.

I wished I felt better about telling him. I didn't get the feeling he hated me, not even a little bit, but I knew he was disappointed. It lowered my spirits to do the right thing and know it still wasn't a good thing. I hoped this didn't turn out to be the main feeling I had of growing up.

"How'd your daddy take it?" Mom asked.

I shrugged.

Mom said, "He regrets what he did. That's hard on him."

"A lot of good that does now," I muttered.

"He's never going to throw anybody else out," Mom said.

"He sleeps in Collin's room," I said. "Maybe *he's* going to move out."

Dolly started biting her nails, making a hard clicking sound, like she was chipping wood.

"We were angry," Mom said, trying to ignore Dolly. "It was too important to both of us to let the subject drop. It seemed the best way to get through something that was very hard on both of us. On all of us."

"What about now?"

"Your daddy and I may always disagree about this. I hope he'll come to a place where he can accept Collin's actions, and mine. Especially mine."

"You mean you'll tell him you're sorry you helped Collin?" I asked, thinking Dolly must have fingernails as thick as linoleum. "If that's what he wants to hear? Dolly, will you quit that?"

"Sorry."

"I did what seemed right to me," Mom said. "I can't help how anybody else feels about it. Not even you or your daddy."

"What if I said that to you?" I asked.

After a moment, Mom said, "You probably will, over something. Most people come to that place with their parents. I hope it won't be too soon."

"Would I love you as much, if I didn't care what you think?"

Mom was quiet for a while. But I could hear my heartbeat, like it was in my ears.

Then Mom said, "It hurts me to go against you and your daddy, even when it—maybe especially because it's to help Collin."

"You have a soft spot for Collin."

"I have a soft spot for you too."

I felt tears coming on, and I busied myself with getting ready for bed to keep from crying. There was the warning of a cool night in the air. "You know what I want? Thick flannel pajamas. They sound so good. Can we get some when we go school shopping?"

"Sure," Mom said.

Dolly asked Mom, "Were you afraid Collin would get killed if he went over there?" I realized it was never my mother she bothered with her questions. Until now.

"Partly. Only partly," Mom said.

"Since Willie left," Dolly said, "we're all afraid. All of us, afraid for him. But also, because nothing will ever be the same again for any of us if he gets hurt. I know it's a lot worse for Willie. I wish he had gotten the idea to run off to Canada."

My held-back tears got away from me. Mom pulled the sheet back on the bed, where she sat and wiped her eyes with the corner.

"I wonder if they'll find each other," Dolly said. "Collin and Thatcher, I mean." Hers were the only dry eyes. I figured her for cried out.

Mom said, "Let's hope they can."

We rustled around, getting comfortable. I lay quiet, listening to the others breathe. A question popped into my head. "What did you do about his winter coat?"

"I took it over with me," Mom said. "Kerrie had a backpack. We stuffed it in there."

We were quiet again, and then Mom spoke up. "Dolly, I haven't had a minute alone with your mother to ask her about Willie."

"He's been there three months and some, so we're going on four, now," Dolly said. "Momma marks off the days on a calendar. She can tell you to the hour, from day to day."

I didn't think Mom was asking how long had Willie been there, but that was what was on Dolly's mind at the moment. Maybe it told Mom all she needed to know.

I knew they had to be there one year exactly, so I understood about the calendar. I couldn't help a little twinge of something, though, a hope that we weren't going to have such a calendar.

"Four months is a third, and a third is nearly a half," Mom said.

"That's a nice way to look at it," Dolly said.

We fell quiet, but I was already thinking it was two more months to halfway, sixty days to halfway, and I didn't like the sound of that. But Mom was offering baby powder, and Dolly knew enough to say thank you.

"I'm going to let you girls get some sleep," Mom said, standing up. It had gone full dark while we were talking, and I could hardly see her.

"Are you going to go looking for Daddy?"

"I might," she said. "I just might."

"I'll wait up," I said.

"We're not sleepy," Dolly said.

We might not have been sleepy, but Dolly yawned. I figured she was working her way up to a question, so I waited, thoughts still circling in my head. After a while, I realized from the sound of her breathing that she had fallen asleep.

I pretended I was wearing flannel pajamas. When sleep overtook me, I didn't notice.

32 HEAD TO HEAD

The next morning, Daddy said, "I'm taking you and your mother home this evening. We're going to start over."

"I'll be ready," I said, and headed around the house.

Dolly was waiting for me on the steps. "Where's Theo?" I asked her. Daddy's truck was loaded up with things for the house, but a few of my uncles found places to sit in the back, their elbows crooked over the sides. Uncle Milford was among them, minus his green cap.

"He's going along to work on the house," she said, pushing her glasses up on her nose. "I'd rather stay here."

"We'll get stuck babysitting," I warned her.

"They're making oatmeal cookies in the kitchen," she said. "Playing with Hammie is more fun than lugging around a pail of water."

Daddy got into his truck and leaned out of the window. "Got a regular seat for you girls if you want to come along with me," he called.

I went.

Theo was waiting for me on the passenger side of the truck, the door open. He boosted me in. I scooted for the middle, right next to Caboose's jaunty smile. Theo swung up behind me, claiming the window seat. He was wearing Uncle Milford's green cap, or one like it.

"Nice cap," I said to Theo.

"Won it from Uncle Milford at dominoes," he said, and tamped the bill down to keep the sun out of his eyes.

Uncle Mac hailed us from the barn. While he jogged over, Theo hunted up a radio station he liked. "Take me out to the house, will you?" Uncle Mac asked. He was short of breath.

"I believe we're going that way," Daddy said.

"Uncle Mac," Theo said. "You want to sit inside?"

"I'm old, son," Uncle Mac said with a grin. "But I ain't so old I cain't ride in a truck bed." To prove it, he threw a leg over the truck bed, and a couple of my uncles made hooting sounds.

As we started out, Caboose swung his big grin over to me. I said, "Keep your dog breath to yourself please," and being a good dog, he did. He turned to face front.

Daddy took his time, dropping two of his brothers in one field and three of them in another. Their machines were waiting right where someone had left off. Daddy drove slowly enough that we could talk to each other over the rush of wind coming in the windows. It was just that nobody did. Not at first. Theo looked off to the side, like he didn't want to talk.

"What's got you thinking so hard these days, Theo?" Daddy said.

"I came out here because I was taking a lot of flak over Thatcher," Theo said. "School's about to start, so there will only be more of the same. I ain't looking forward to it."

Daddy said, "Guess Thatcher didn't think about that."

"I'm glad he didn't go over there and get himself killed, I guess," Theo said. "Or worse." He was not looking out the window anymore, but at Daddy. "I've got this book Thatcher left behind. It pretty much makes a case for taking the first train to Canada."

"It's one story," Daddy said.

"There's a lot of boys with the same story," Theo said. Something in his voice made me a little afraid. Theo had changed, just as Dolly had done, and I had not realized it till right then.

"Men," Daddy said. "Men, not boys."

"Not on graduation day," Theo said. "You called them boys then. Guess they're all boys till they get broke or die."

I started to wish I had gotten the window seat. Then again, I figured it would be harder for them to come to blows with me and the dog sitting in between.

Daddy said, "You sound mad."

"I am mad," Theo said. The look he'd turned on Daddy did not waver, not even when Daddy looked back. Theo said, "Surely there must be some other way to manage ourselves. We shouldn't have to shoot each other down."

Daddy said, "Men feel differently when they get old enough to look back on everything they worked for. They want to hold on to it, and they want to keep it safe."

"Well, there's an idea," Theo said. "If there are old men in this world who think a fight is so important, then let's see how many other old men they can talk into going with them. See how many wars we get into then."

"Now, that's a young man's way of thinking," Daddy said, getting riled. I started holding my breath.

"If I got old and I couldn't ask somebody else to do my fighting for me," Theo said, "maybe I'd have to figure out another way to solve my problems."

Daddy said, "You know what I think—"

"I want to know what Willie thinks, Uncle Wick," Theo said. "Beg pardon, but it's what Willie's thinking that matters to me right now."

Daddy bit down on anything else he wanted to say. I pretended not to notice. But something about the way Theo talked to Daddy gave me goose bumps. I believed Thatcher would be proud of him too.

Daddy turned down a dirt road, and we rode in to see how things were going at the house. From the outside, it looked like a house, ready to move into. It had doors and some window glass, put in that very morning. Theo went right to where more of the windows were being set in.

He waved to me with the hammer, big boy him. I filled the bucket from the new water faucet and set it where no one would fall over it and nothing like sawdust was likely to fall into it either. I dropped the tin ladle in.

I filled up the bucket we'd carry around to the fields. I slid it back along the truck bed and pulled some other things around it so it wouldn't slosh all over. Job done.

I climbed up the ladder to talk to Theo. I couldn't get up quite as high as he sat—my legs started to feel too weak. "Good going," I said when he finished a nail.

"Aw, I don't want to argue with Uncle Wick," he said, laying his hammer aside. "He's a good guy."

"I liked what you said," I told him. "I wanted to make you feel better, that's all, when I said it was just a book."

"I know it," Theo said. "Except it ain't just a book."

"I just wanted to help."

"Well, you're a good guy too." He grinned and went back to

nailing down a slat. I climbed back down the ladder, my knees shaking. It was mostly the height, but it was also that Theo couldn't fool me. There wasn't enough baby powder in the world; there weren't any words, either, to help Theo. Or Dolly. Or me.

I had never felt helpless before, and it was not an easy feeling to live with. It struck me that Daddy might find it much easier to take a side, to be strong in an opinion, than to feel helpless.

Meanwhile, Daddy had tried the new plumbing from both the kitchen and the bathroom sink, and flushed the toilet. I followed him around as he flicked light switches on and off, even where the lights hadn't been put in yet. Uncle Mac touched a bulb with two wires sticking out of the end to the wires that stuck out of the wall, and when the lightbulb went on, it was pronounced good.

When I got tired of these marvels, I walked over to check the garden. The barrel had been moved, and there was no sign of the baby rabbits.

"We saw them when we came over here last evening," Uncle Mac said as he walked past me. "Playing around over there under that vine with the big flat leaves. They were clumsy. Wobbly. Like Stellie."

I sat down to watch for them, but it wasn't another two minutes before Daddy was ready to go. "Theo's staying here. Where's the dog?" he asked me.

I shrugged. "He's probably found a shady place for a nap."

"Let's go," Daddy said. "Somebody'll bring him on back to the farm."

I climbed into the truck. We hadn't gotten fifty yards before Caboose was running along behind us, barking. Daddy stopped and let him climb in, swearing as Caboose hooked Daddy's brake leg with his claws. With a noisy scrabble of toenails, he made it aboard and took his usual seat in the middle. He panted and drooled, the picture of dog joy.

"Keep your dog breath to yourself," I told him. But I scratched him between the ears.

As we turned onto the main road, a truck carrying a load of live chickens to market passed us. The wind whipped through those cages, leaving a milky way of feathers trailing behind. Daddy's truck filled with the odor of chicken dirt, and a flurry of yellowed feathers settled on the seats and over us.

I brushed the feathers away as soon as they touched me.

"And you thought dog breath was a terrible thing," Daddy said.

When I didn't give him the grin he was looking for, he said, "I don't want you taking too much of what Theo said to heart."

I didn't think it would help matters to tell Daddy I was hoping he had. "Theo and Dolly think these things over all the time," I said. "It's real for them."

"Well, of course it's real," Daddy said. His face went dark. "Do you think I have forgotten what it means to lose somebody you love?"

"Don't yell at me," I said.

"All right, I'm sorry," Daddy said. "But I don't know how you could say that. It wasn't all that long ago that Pop died. Maybe you were too young then, maybe that's it."

"That's *not* it," I said. "I remember when Pop died." Now I was getting mad. I wanted to say, Pop died in his sleep, that's different. I thought Daddy ought to know that, I really did.

I didn't know how to argue it like Theo, but Daddy was wrong if he didn't think there was a difference. I wanted to say something that made his insides cringe, like when Dolly cried about Willie getting shot to bits, but I didn't know how to make it come out right. I didn't know how to make it flicker on the backs of his eyelids, the way it did on mine.

"I think we have to take it to heart," I told him finally. "It hurts people to ignore the things that are happening to them."

He didn't answer this, but pulled off the road onto the tractor path a little before the usual place. I braced my feet on the dashboard so I wouldn't bounce all over. The dog had his own method. Caboose sat that seat like a sack of sand, his insides shifting around for balance.

"What're they doing, horsing around over there?" Daddy said as we came over the ridge. It wasn't what he said, it was his tone of voice that got my attention. I sat straighter on the seat, trying to see over the nose of the truck.

33 FOREVER FALLING

Uncle Milford and my cousin Vernon, who was sixteen, ran alongside the sickle bar mower. It looked like they were playing tag. Dolly's dad, sitting deep in the noise, took no notice of them but drove on through the row.

Uncle Milford dropped like he'd run into a wall, fell out of sight.

Vernon stopped still, picture of a boy in the sunlight, and Dolly's dad drove on, slow and steady as time. In my mind's eye I saw Uncle Milford fall again. And again. Each time more slowly.

Daddy jammed his foot down on the gas pedal. I clung to the seat, one arm thrown over the back and one hand glued to the door handle. I kept my eyes on the spot where Uncle Milford fell, willing him to get up and start running again. Vernon didn't move, even as we pulled to a stop behind him.

Daddy jumped out of the truck, and I stayed right behind him. Caboose started to bark as soon as he hit the ground, and nobody tried to shush him.

"Your belt," Daddy yelled at Vernon. "Your belt, Vernon. Give it to me." He dropped to his knees next to Uncle Milford.

"I don't know how it happened, Uncle Wick." Vernon began

to cry as he fumbled with the buckle. "We were playing around. I didn't think he was so close to the blades."

Uncle Milford's right pants leg ended in a bright red band that grew wider as I looked on. He didn't say anything, only watched all of us.

Daddy snatched at Vernon's belt, nearly yanking him off his feet as it snapped free. Daddy's hands were fast and sure, not shaking the way Vernon's did. He pulled the belt tight around Uncle Milford's leg, up near the top.

At the end of the row, Dolly's dad turned and started back. He sped up when he saw there was trouble. The mower turned faster.

Everything happened fast, but my eyes took nothing for granted. I saw everything so completely, it seemed to be in slow motion. Caboose had worn down to a hoarse frenzied bark. Vernon looked so chalky, I thought he'd pass out.

Daddy yelled at him, but the racketing of the mower drowned out all other sound. Even Caboose's voice disappeared. Daddy strained to pull the belt tighter, sweat dripping off his face like rainwater. Vernon reached down to help him.

Everything went silent—the machinery stopped. Caboose stopped barking. Something beat in my ears where the sound of the mower left off.

Dolly's dad jumped off the tractor and ran to us. Daddy said, "Let's get him into the truck."

They did it, maybe they even did it well. Things were going quickly again. Uncle Milford still had not made a sound.

I climbed into the back after Vernon slammed up the tailgate and grabbed Uncle Milford by one hand. Dolly's dad would drive and got Caboose into the truck with a whistle.

Daddy planted his feet against Uncle Milford's hip and pulled tight on the belt, signaling Vernon to take over. He was a strong boy.

Daddy pulled off his shirt, bunching it up under Uncle Milford's head as the truck began to move. Then he shifted back to help Vernon.

I braced myself against the side of the truck and clung to Uncle Milford's hand as if I could keep him there by needing him so much. He squeezed back. "It's all right, Grace," he said in a thin voice. "It doesn't hurt."

"That's it," Daddy told Vernon. "It's all but stopped."

"I can hold it." Vernon no sooner said that than we hit a rut, and a fresh flow of blood spread over the floor of the truck. Vernon pulled tight again. It was then that I saw the tears in Daddy's eyes.

One sob escaped me. I sucked myself back inside, letting silent tears roll down my face.

"Uncle Wick. You know what he said when he fell? 'It's cut clean off, isn't it, Vernon?' Just like that, Uncle Wick, without so much as a twitch of his eyebrow."

"I'm thirsty," Uncle Milford said. His voice sounded cracked.

Daddy slid the water bucket across, sloshing water over the truck bed. It washed through enough blood to run red by the time it got to the other end of the truck. Daddy looked stricken, but he didn't say anything. He filled the ladle, then lifted Uncle Milford's head to help him drink.

Vernon wiped one hand on his jeans and went for a better grip, pulling until Uncle Milford's face showed pain.

"Hurting some?" Daddy said.

"Feels achy," Uncle Milford said.

"We'll be there soon now," Daddy said.

"Wick," Uncle Milford said. "Am I going to die?"

Daddy's eyebrows knitted together in a frown. "Why, no, Milford, I don't think so."

I didn't know whether to believe Daddy or not. Uncle Milford's skin looked dry and thickened somehow. His coloring was the worst. Gray. "Are you doing okay, Uncle Milford?" I asked him.

"I'm feeling a little poorly, sweetheart," he said. His hand trembled when he tried to give mine a squeeze.

Daddy moved back to Vernon and helped him tighten the belt. It took the two of them to manage as well as either one of them did at first.

"Wick?" Uncle Milford said.

"Yeah?"

"Just in case, Wick . . . I want you to tell Ma . . . I love her. Tell my sweetheart . . ."

"Milford, you're going to be all right. We're nearly there."

"Just needed . . . you tell them . . ."

"Uncle Wick?" Vernon's fear was in his voice.

Daddy shook his head, warning off the question.

Fresh tears rolled down Vernon's face as he reset his grip on the belt. It couldn't be pulled any tighter, but Uncle Milford didn't flinch.

It gave me some relief to feel a weak response when I squeezed his hand.

Dolly's dad pulled into Doc Petersen's driveway, continuing across the lawn, where the doctor rose from his flower bed wearing a cotton apron. He came over the side of the truck, and I let go of Uncle Milford's hand to get out of the way.

Dolly's dad and Vernon readied themselves to carry Uncle

Milford inside. The doctor sat quiet, a finger pressed to Uncle Milford's throat. He shifted his hand to another spot and pressed again.

Uncle Milford's hand lay where I dropped it, still curved to hold mine.

"The boy's gone, Wick. I'm sorry."

I knew only the long slow fall of my heart. Uncle Milford wasn't there to catch me.

34 FAMILY REUNION

My aunts and uncles and their children scattered across the lawn with paper plates and iced tea. It looked like a regular day, except that the men wore their church-going hats and ties, looking taller somehow with their jackets flapping in the breeze and their hair slicked to the side.

The women were in their Sunday best, wearing white gloves. Uncle Milford's girl stood among them. Slow tears had been running down her cheeks for so long that the deep collar of her dress stuck to her like wet paper.

Once we were back from the cemetery, Dolly hung close to her momma. I got the feeling she thought her momma needed watching over. Theo went off by himself. I had no desire to go along. I wanted a kind of privacy myself, just not so far away from the rest of the family that I was actually alone.

Everyone tried to talk about something besides losing Uncle Milford. They concentrated on what they had ahead of them for the next few days. Some of my uncles talked about finishing the house before cold weather set in—no use letting it go to waste.

I heard Uncle Mac talking about the farm machinery he

planned to see at the state fair, if he managed to catch the last two days. Dolly's dad talked about the price of feed.

The little'ns ran around like it was any other old day. Watching their antics brought out a few shadowy smiles.

Late in the afternoon, Daddy called out to Aunt Birdie to come into the house to help him with something. This caused no one to take notice, except that Aunt Birdie did go right in.

It was only because I went in for another pitcher of sweet tea and I heard Daddy say to Aunt Birdie in the gentlest way, "We got a call from Sawyer, Birdie. He's on the phone and wants to talk to you" that I knew anything special was going on.

This was too much for Aunt Birdie, who cried through the whole call. She probably couldn't even hear Uncle Sawyer. It was too much for me as well, and I ducked into that fit-for-a-queen bathroom to wail into a towel.

Only once I was able to go back outside did I get the story. Uncle Sawyer and two other fellows had made their way through the jungle to some base camp, and were coming home.

It was only after Daddy had first told Dolly's folks and then tried to find Grandma to tell her that he told us the rest. The doctors wanted to clear up an infection in Uncle Sawyer's foot before they shipped him back. It might be months before we saw him.

It was hard, these things coming together. Nobody knew whether to cry from pain or joy. Aunt Lutie wondered how Aunt Birdie would manage if Uncle Sawyer wasn't well. It was decided that he would put up in Aunt Mayfred's spare room if he needed special care. She lived only a short walk down the road from Aunt Birdie.

I heard Dolly's dad say Uncle Sawyer might come to regret

that—Aunt Mayfred could talk the feathers off a chicken. There was some shaky laughter to follow this comment, even from Aunt Mayfred.

Daddy went on to tell everyone that Collin was on his way to Canada. He said he hoped everyone would understand that our boys were men now, and would be making their own decisions. He hoped everyone would be able to respect Collin and Thatcher for theirs, just as we all respected Uncle Sawyer's and Willie's decision to serve.

My heart beat harder when I realized what he was telling us, and somehow, although I was afraid, I was proud too. There was a moment or two when no one said anything. Then Aunt Chloris said she felt like having a little more of that sheet cake, could she get some for anybody else?

I found myself wanting to find a corner to hide in. It wasn't shame. I was grateful to find I didn't feel ashamed of Collin, but I needed some time alone to take everything in.

I ducked around to the front of the house and passed a couple of my aunts who were just inside the front porch, talking quietly while they rubbed their babies' backs to put them to sleep. I kept on going, heading for the far side of the house, for the nearest bunkhouse.

Grandma was inside. She knew I had come in, but she went on smoothing the cotton slip over the pillow. It was quiet here in a way that made me feel welcomed. I recognized the empty space where Uncle Milford used to be immediately.

"What's going on out there?" Grandma asked me.

"Daddy told everyone that Collin has gone to Canada," I said. I didn't feel able to tell her about Uncle Sawyer.

"Well, that's all right then," Grandma said. "It's best to have these things out in the open."

"It's what Mom wanted," I said. "She wanted Collin to be safe. I wanted that too, but I don't know—I thought Uncle Milford was going to be safe here."

"There's no promise of safety in any life, Grace," Grandma said. "It doesn't matter what your momma wanted. Or your daddy, because I can guess why he's been going around like he has a thorn in his heel. What counts now is what Collin wanted."

"It's hard to be sure," I said. "No one agrees, and they all feel so strongly that they are right."

Grandma said, "That's why every one of these boys has to do what they feel is right for themselves alone."

I wanted to tell her about Uncle Sawyer, and maybe I would have if I'd found her anywhere else. I stood there, my chest so tight it pained me, but I took the first really deep breath I'd managed in two days.

"He slept here, Grace, from the day he turned six," Grandma said. "I'd come out here every night to see my boys was warm, and I can remember each of their faces, in the moonlight, faces so little and sweet."

I felt better just hearing Grandma sound so sure of herself. She wasn't taking sides exactly, and it didn't sound to me like anyone could be entirely wrong, no matter what they did.

Grandma spread her hand over a corner of the pillow, crushing it till her knuckles showed white. She swallowed noisily.

I bent to stretch my arms around her shoulders, reaching to cross them in front the way I'd seen Uncle Milford do so often, and squeezed her up in a hug. A little whimper escaped her, and

I felt her tears on my wrist. In spite of being different from anything I'd ever done, it felt right, the way Grandma and I fit together.

"Grace. Honey." Her voice was hardly a sigh. "I don't know that I ever told Milford how it warmed me to have one of my boys so affectionate in his ways." She began to cry. "I don't know how I'll face the mornings."

"You'll have family all around you, Grandma," I said. "We will all put our arms around you."

I had learned this best from Uncle Milford. Family was there to catch you.

35 A BROKEN HEART

I went home with Mom and Daddy after Uncle Milford's funeral.

Mom and I did my school shopping, and then school started.

Daddy spent a little more time at the mill, and at suppertime he talked about stuff like the grass needed mowing, the truck needed to be inspected.

Mom put a big cloth over the buffet and started painting a little table. The loss we felt over Uncle Milford's death had gotten all tangled up with our feelings about Collin. We didn't talk much about either one.

Judy took the news about Collin very hard. "But you know where he is, right?" she asked. "Secretly, I mean. You do know."

I shook my head.

"I swear I won't tell a soul. Not even my mother."

"We don't know, Judy. He hasn't written, he hasn't called."

"Don't you miss him?"

I nodded. What I couldn't tell her was, I'd begun to enjoy the feeling of missing Collin. She'd never understand.

I wasn't mad at him anymore, not for going. Not the way I would have been if he'd stayed and Mom and Daddy kept fighting over him. This way I'd had a chance to find out there were things I liked about him.

If he came home now, I would still like those things, even if I got mad at him sometimes for acting like a brother. It was good to find that out. I hoped he was going to get to come home. Someday.

"You've never appreciated him," Judy complained while I tried to figure out how to answer her.

That girl is chock-full of surprises. "Did you?" I asked.

"Oh, Grace, you don't get it. You aren't interested in boys. And he was your brother. I know that makes a difference."

"I'm interested in boys," I said, feeling a little insulted.

"Oh, I know," Judy said, rolling her eyes. "You were interested in sitting next to Lonnie O'Toole in biology because he'd want to be the one who dissected the frog."

So right. If I sat with Judy, the way she wanted, I would have had to do the hard part. But I liked boys. It had nothing to do with frogs. I didn't advertise it when I liked a boy, that's all. If Judy had a brother, she'd know how boys could talk about girls who like them. She wouldn't like that either.

"Judy?" I said when she started to cry. "What is it?"

"I have loved Collin since I was eight years old," she wailed, "and now, when I'm reaching an age where he might take me seriously, he's gone! It is so unfair."

Collin would never have taken an interest in her, at least not the kind of interest she had in mind. But it seemed cruel to say so. He was, after all, gone. "Why didn't you ever tell me?" I asked.

She snorted, spraying tears all over me. At least I hoped it was all tears. Anyway, it was news to me that Collin had in some way made Judy love him. I tried to think what he might have done.

"He always took you seriously," I said. That much was true.

He never wanted to date her, that's all. "He liked your sense of humor. Really. He liked you much better than he liked me."

"Thanks for saying that."

"Mom says the war won't last forever. And maybe then . . ." Mom couldn't bear to think he would never come home. And lately, neither could I. Because I had learned, things change.

I thought about Collin a lot, wondering what he thought when he found my money in his pocket. I hoped he needed it, because I certainly missed seeing it in my drawer. Then again, I hoped he didn't need it too much.

I was glad he had his jacket. Because it got cold right after Labor Day, as usual. Mom took to listening to the radio, trying different stations, trying to get weather reports from farther north.

Then I woke in the middle of one night.

36 EARLY MORNING CHILL

It wasn't noise that woke me but the sound of someone moving too quietly. They'd shut my bedroom door. I got up, my heart beating hard and fast, to look out into the hall. No one was there, but I could hear the scrape of Caboose's toenails as he got to the bottom of the stairs.

I hurried right along behind. I don't know that I thought Collin had come home. Sneaked home. I don't know what I might have done if he had, whether or not I'd have called out to Mom and Daddy. It was a relief to find it was only my mother I was following.

She'd heard me coming and was waiting at the bottom of the stairs in her sleep shirt, flashlight in hand. She carried her jeans and a plaid shirt over one arm. She whispered, "What are you doing up at this hour?"

"Wondering the same thing about you," I whispered back, sinking my fingers into the fur of the dog's ruff as he came to lean against me. Caboose made himself a resting place for any hand that didn't have something better to do. He wriggled with excitement.

Mom put a finger to her lips, listened a moment, then motioned for me to follow her into the kitchen. "I have an errand to run," she told me in a low voice.

"It isn't light yet," I said as she pulled the jeans on. It was cold in the kitchen too.

"I'm taking Caboose with me." The plaid shirt was going on over her sleep shirt. "You go on back to bed and stay there."

My jacket hung on a hook behind the door. "I'm going with you," I said, pulling my jacket on over my flannel pajamas.

It wasn't just that Mom was doing something I didn't understand. Or because she was going without telling me where. It was her shoes. She slipped her feet into scuffed white tennis shoes without first putting on socks. I had never before seen Mom put her bare feet into these shoes.

Finally, apart from the shoes, this was the first time she'd seemed like herself in so long, I wanted to be with her. I wouldn't take no for an answer. I was right behind Caboose. "Don't let the screen door slam behind you," Mom warned me.

"Where are the two of you going?" Daddy asked from the hallway. Mom and I froze in place. He came into the kitchen and stared at both of us, first questioning, and then letting it dawn on him. And on me.

This had something to do with Collin.

"Wick," Mom said. It was that high-pitched voice.

"Go on, then," he said. "If I make pancakes for breakfast, will you be back in time to have some?"

"Half an hour," Mom said. "Maybe a little longer."

"You have a soft spot where that boy is concerned," Daddy said, pointing at Mom.

"I hope so," she said.

Daddy reached for the coffeepot, and Mom stepped off the porch.

"Wait for me," I said, and ran back upstairs to snatch Collin's cap out from under my dresser. Then I beat it back downstairs.

Daddy stopped me before I could make it out the door. He held out a wad of bills. "Everything I have in the house," he said. "Tell your mom to send it on. Tell her we want a phone call to know he got it."

"Right," I said, and ducked away.

Mom waited in the car. It wasn't in the driveway but out on the street. I ran across the lawn and got in, glad suddenly that this old car always had to be warmed up. I sat up front, a privilege I enjoyed more frequently since Collin had gone. I hadn't often done it in pajamas.

There were two cardboard boxes and a battered suitcase in the back. Caboose took up what was left of the backseat. He put his paws up as if to jump to the front. "Sit," I said, and he did.

"Here," I said, handing Mom the money. "Daddy says he wants a phone call that says it got there."

Mom opened the glove compartment, put in a small brown-paper-wrapped package and stuffed the money under it.

"So where are we going?" I asked once we were on our way.

"I don't want to talk about it," Mom said.

In recent weeks I'd come to know this meant she didn't want to argue about it. Well, me neither. I had slapped a lot of the dust off Collin's cap as I ran, and I finished picking it clean.

Lately, we talked about Collin in lowered voices, and more often, didn't mention his name to each other for days at all. I doubt any of us ever stopped thinking about him. All else had dropped away.

The town was dark, the streets empty. It had rained during the night. I'd come through here after dark before, but I'd never seen it like this—eerie with mists rising from the blacktop. I was glad I'd come along; I was also glad we had Caboose with us.

"Why are we stopping here?" I asked as my mother pulled over to the curb in front of the Rexall drugstore. Caboose put his forepaws over the back of the car seat and leaned over my shoulder. "Sit," I told him.

But Mom turned around and grabbed his fur at both sides of his head and rubbed her face against his, saying all manner of sweet things to him, baby-talking him. "What a good boy is Boo," she said. "Good boy. Sweet Boo." I hadn't seen her treat him quite like this since he was a puppy.

I was shocked to see tears in her eyes. Not that she didn't love Caboose—we all did. And of course, every time we looked at him, we wondered about Collin. "Mom?"

"I'm sending Caboose to Canada," she said.

My breath caught. "You *do* know where Collin is, then."

"He asked a friend to let us know he's all right. Nothing more. If I send Caboose—" She couldn't say any more. She kept swallowing hard, swallowing down tears.

Before either of us could say anything more, a pickup truck rattled around the corner and pulled into the parking space in front of us. I saw two people in the truck; it was Danny Taggart who got out. He'd been on the softball team with Collin.

His denim jacket was painted with peace symbols. "Hi, Mrs. Whitaker," he said as Mom rolled down the window. Cold air rushed in. "Grace," he said when he saw me.

"Hey," I said, hugging my knees to keep warm.

Mom took the package out of the glove compartment. "Put this in a safe place, Danny," she said. It had been taped all the way around twice to protect it, and she'd written our name and address all over it. I figured it was money.

"Here," I said, grabbing the other money Daddy gave me. "Tell Collin Daddy sent it and that he wants Collin to call home."

"That'll be good news," Danny said. He shoved both the money and the box deep into his pants pocket.

Mom asked, "Do you know where you're going to be staying?"

"Don't worry," Danny said. "It's relatives all the way. My aunt in Chicago, and Leon has folks in Minnesota. We'll be fine." He opened the back door.

Caboose did not need to be coaxed, and danced around the street, hind end a-wagging. "Wanna go for a ride, fella? Wanna see ol' Coll?" Danny said to him.

"When you get to Canada—" Mom began as she got out of the car.

"We plan to stop at a kind of safe house. They're Americans, an older couple. Then we'll go on to Coll's place and stay with him till we find jobs. He says there's a meat-packing plant in town. We plan to stick close to each other till this is over."

"Here's a leash for Caboose," Mom said. "Not that he's likely to cooperate with you if you actually try to use it."

"We'll take good care of him," Danny said, and he hugged my mom, a sight I never thought I'd see. I couldn't imagine Collin wanting to hug Danny's mom. And then, like he was in a hurry, Danny said, "Is this other stuff to go too?"

"How are your parents with this?" Mom asked shakily.

"Mom's okay," Danny said. "Dad'll come around in a decade

or two." His voice cracked on *decade*. He said to me, "Collin said to tell you he loves you and he misses you."

Until recently I didn't think big boys cried anymore. Whether it was the sound of tears in his voice, or the message from Collin, or that I'd begun to feel too much of what was happening here, I got a tearing pain in my heart that was all about Collin.

Mom said, "I have a bag of dog food in the trunk."

"That's a mom for you," Danny said, wiping his eyes. "Thinks of everything."

"Hey, I nearly forgot," I said, reaching out the window. "Take this cap to Collin, will you?"

Leon Wentworth had gotten out of their truck by then, and he put the cap on his own head. Leon was the last kid I expected to see on his way to Canada. He wasn't the kind of kid Collin and Danny Taggart hung around with. He wasn't involved in sports. He always had a paperback book in his hip pocket when he worked at the grocery store after school.

He still had—I saw the bulge in his pocket when he turned to put Collin's stuff into the back of the pickup. Caboose jumped up into the back of the truck and settled himself as cheerfully as he'd gotten into our car, letting his tongue loll with contentment.

I noticed again how quiet everything was, the feel of damp in the air. There were lights coming on, the town had begun waking up, but no one had yet looked any further than putting on slippers and starting coffee.

Warning them to be careful driving, Mom hugged both boys. It didn't seem so strange this time. Still, I could hardly believe what I was hearing. Witnessing. Danny and Leon were running off the way Collin did—to stay with Collin, it sounded like.

Mom stood outside the car until they'd pulled away, turned a corner, and were out of sight. Still she stood there, like she was leaning a little into the wind, only there wasn't any. It all seemed to have happened very quickly.

I watched the empty street too, suddenly remembering how short I'd been with Caboose, telling him to sit, and never reaching back to pat him when he finally did. He'd always been such a good dog, and I hadn't had time to say good-bye.

A desperate longing fluttered in my chest. It felt just like having a bird trapped in there, frightened and wanting to be free. "Mom," I said, and it came out almost like a moan, making me sorry immediately, I felt so stupid.

But she came and got into the car, her eyes shining, her face pinched with all that she was holding back, and said, "I hope he's going to be okay there."

I said, "Don't worry. Collin doesn't have the knack for trouble."

37 THE RIGHT FEELING

Mom ran her hands through her hair once it was too late to call them back, the way she does when she feels things have gotten away from her. When she thinks things are too broken to fix. She started the car, saying, "Right at this moment I'm very grateful to have you here."

"You sent Collin money, didn't you? The little package?"

"It was his money." By that she meant the money she'd made him save from his pay. She'd taken it out of the bank for him.

"Well, Daddy sent him a couple hundred dollars, I think," I said.

Mom said, "I'll talk to your daddy when we get home. I want him to know you had nothing to do with planning this."

"Why didn't you tell Daddy where we were going?" I asked as we turned onto our street. "He was right there."

"I wanted to. But Danny's mother trusted me with his secret. I couldn't take a chance your daddy would say something to Danny's father."

My anger took Mom by surprise. It took me by surprise. "You thought Daddy would tell?"

"He doesn't like what our family is going through, Grace. He might think it was only right—"

I said, "Like he thought it was right for Collin to go to war."

She gave me a look that meant I'd said enough. "Maybe things will be better now," she said. "Knowing Collin's safe. That's why I sent Caboose. So Collin would have a little piece of home too."

"Did you ever think Daddy might have liked to help? He might have liked to make up for before?"

"I promised Danny's mom. Mothers and fathers see this differently," Mom said. "Mothers have to stick together on this."

I understood. Sad to say, but I did.

Daddy had breakfast waiting. It felt strange to walk into the warmth of the kitchen, with the sweet smells of pancakes and syrup and no one speaking. We sat down and ate in silence. It wasn't all that bad. There wasn't any feeling of anyone about to blow a gasket or anything. Caboose wasn't there to beg for bacon—that was a little hard.

Only when we had finished, Daddy said, "Are you going to tell me about it?"

"What Collin's done is done," Mom said, "and we may never agree about it. I don't want to ask that of you anymore."

"We have to do things differently from here on out," Daddy said. "I think we still have to do them like we've done most things. Together."

"I didn't want him to die over there," Mom said. "I didn't want to spend the rest of my life wondering whether he suffered, whether he died alone."

Daddy said, "The next time you're going to need to do something like this, talk to me. Give me a chance to be included."

Mom looked like it was the last thing she expected him to say. "Thank you, Wick," she said in a near whisper.

38 HAPPY BIRTHDAY TO ME

On a warm day in the fall, I came home from school to find Mom sitting on the porch swing. I sat there too, and looked more closely at things I didn't used to notice so much. Colors were brighter or darker, and some things I'd seen so many times in my whole life that they had become invisible suddenly looked new to me. It wasn't only the change of seasons, but because we were different somehow.

It wasn't all bad, it was just that it was all different. I wanted something that felt old and comfortable. The pajamas were good, but they didn't quite do it.

"Collin called today," Mom said. "He said he's okay. He said Caboose made the trip very well."

Her voice sounded thick, so I didn't ask her right away to tell me everything he said. Besides, I was afraid my own voice might sound the same way. I wanted Caboose in the worst way sometimes, but I kept shut about it. I could hardly admit, even to myself, to missing Collin in a distant way. But I really wanted to have Caboose right back where I could dig my fingers into his fur.

Well, once I did say something about it.

I told Mom, "I feel bad for Caboose. Collin at least understands why he's someplace different."

Mom laughed. She said, "Caboose loves your brother. He's happy there."

I went on missing the dog while we sat there on the swing, but I thought we'd said all there was to say. If I brought it up, Mom was likely to think of some way to make me say I loved Collin.

"I found these in Collin's room when I was packing for him," Mom said. "It didn't seem like the right time to show them to you." She held out two little boxes. "I didn't want to make you feel more caught between a rock and a hard place than you already did."

I couldn't help but smile. Not at the two tiny wrapped presents, but at Mom, saying *a rock and a hard place*. She had been spending a lot of time out at Grandma's, that was for sure.

I opened them already knowing what I would find, and only half believing it. The first charm was a tiny bicycle with wheels that really turned. The second was the little ballerina—not that I had ever taken a dance class, or wanted to, that I could remember. But the little spray of tulle that was her skirt broke my heart with wanting to be so precious.

Suddenly, I felt I was. Precious. In some weird, probably warped big boy way, Collin held me precious. Enough to spend a hunk of his paycheck on these charms. Or on the other ones, anyway. The little birthday cake and *party!*

Those charms had been left to rattle around in the corner of one of my drawers. But now I knew how he'd meant them to be seen. As mementos of my first boys-and-girls-together party.

Whatever made him burn his draft card that day, he had not been thinking of spoiling my fun. He had been on my side the whole time I was begging and bargaining for a party.

"You know, you don't have to have a birthday to throw a party," Mom said.

"No?"

"You can just want to have a good time," she said. "That's what Collin said about your birthday party."

"Let's get the other charms," I said. They'd been in a corner of my sock drawer since my birthday. "Will you help me put them on the bracelet?"

"I'll get those skinny pliers your daddy has in the garage," Mom said.

Holding those charms gave me the exact feeling I wanted from my flannel pajamas. Wearing them on the bracelet would do the same thing. I would need that till Collin came home.

ACKNOWLEDGMENTS

With each book, I am ever more astonished at the number of people it takes to bring a book to the readers. This is not because there are so many Roles to be Fulfilled, which is enough to amaze, but because there would be so many open holes in the fabric of the thing without—not just the Supreme Efforts, and there are many of those—but the Chance and Discovery and Sheer Luck of the right words, coming from someone else of course, that are simply the answer I needed at the time.

I'm so grateful to Jennifer Flannery, the agent for this book, for a letter that detailed what she loved about the story. It helped when I forgot what *I* loved about the story.

I'm grateful to Kathy Dawson, my editor, for staying with me during the several long dips into a previously neglected well of memory that will probably generate many more stories. But it didn't make this one any easier on either of us to deliver.

And to her assistant, Nicole Kasprzak, who knew right where to find a telling piece of information, seemed to yank it right out of the universe, when we needed it in the final hour.

To say nothing of "if." Thanks, Nicole.

Every writer is only as good as the advice she's offered when things aren't going well—from fellow writers, Miriam Brenaman, Uma Krishnaswami, Susan Krawitz, Carol Shank, Pat Richards, Debbie Hoskins, Catherine Bieberich, Katie Beatty, Jenni Holm! Smart women who all addressed different issues, I cannot thank you enough. See you all at the SCBWI conference in L.A. Can I be the one with the cell phone?

Plus, thank you Susan and Hannah, for keeping my dog sane.

Last, never least, I thank my husband, Akila, from the seat of my soul for his boundless support. I will fan you with palm leaves for the rest of our lives. How about a foot massage? Anything, honey.